THE MOUTH OF DOOM

"Who wants to be the first victim of the Haunted Holiday ride?" Jason asked.

"I'll go," Joe offered. He climbed into the coffin's red crushed-velvet seat.

The coffin plunged into a lofty crypt, and the ghostly apparition of a woman in a lace gown appeared. "Help me!" she cried, reaching out for him.

"Sorry, lady," Joe tossed back to her.

Suddenly the entrance to the tunnel was illuminated, revealing the huge head of a vampire. The track disappeared into the vampire's mouth.

"Cool," Joe said, bracing himself for the plunge into the entrance.

As Joe's coffin approached, the teeth began to close. Each fang was at least three feet long and coated with a metallic finish. Joe knew it was just a ride, but still he ducked lower in the coffin.

The next thing he saw was the vampire's fang as it fell like a guillotine, tearing through the wood of his coffin!

Nancy Drew & Hardy Boys SuperMysteries

Available from ARCHWAY Paperbacks

A NANCY DREW and HARDY BOYS
SUPER·MYSTERY™

HOLLYWOOD HORROR

Carolyn Keene

AN ARCHWAY PAPERBACK
Published by POCKET BOOKS
New York London Toronto Sydney Tokyo Singapore

Ingram 9/15/94 # 3.99

This book is a work of fiction. Names, characters, places and incidents are products of the author's imagination or are used fictitiously. Any resemblance to actual events or locales or persons, living or dead, is entirely coincidental.

AN ARCHWAY PAPERBACK *Original*

An Archway Paperback published by
POCKET BOOKS, a division of Simon & Schuster Inc.
1230 Avenue of the Americas, New York, NY 10020

Copyright © 1994 by Simon & Schuster Inc.
Produced by Mega-Books, Inc.

ISBN: 0-671-78181-2

First Archway Paperback printing October 1994

10 9 8 7 6 5 4 3 2 1

NANCY DREW, THE HARDY BOYS, AN ARCHWAY
PAPERBACK and colophon are registered trademarks of
Simon & Schuster Inc.

A NANCY DREW AND HARDY BOYS SUPERMYSTERY
is a trademark of Simon & Schuster Inc.

Cover art by Vince Natale

Printed in the U.S.A.

IL 6+

HOLLYWOOD
HORROR

Chapter

One

Eeeeooow!" Nancy Drew's scream pierced the darkness as the rocket she was riding in veered wildly toward a massive meteor.

"We're going to crash!" cried Bess Marvin, Nancy's friend.

"Hold on!" Nancy felt a tingle of fear as she clutched the safety bar in front of her. She'd been on some thrilling amusement park rides before, but this voyage through cosmic galaxies took her breath away!

Just when a collision seemed inevitable, the meteor exploded, sending fragments of matter scattering through the darkness of deep space. The rocket plunged into the wake of the blast, and there was a flash of orange light, followed by thick white mist that cooled Nancy's skin.

1

"Mission accomplished!" a voice boomed over a loudspeaker as the rocket swept into a sea of royal blue lit by twinkling stars.

"Easy for you to say." Joe Hardy mocked the voice as the rocket slowed and descended into a series of gentle loops. "That voice has been bugging me since we blasted off from planet X."

"I didn't mind the voice," said Joe's older brother, Frank. "It was those gooey orange-and-green aliens on Zebular that turned my stomach."

"I loved every minute of Space Race," Nancy said.

"Me, too!" Bess agreed. "It was just like the movie."

"Every ride here is based on a movie that HG Studios produced," Frank explained as their rocket pulled up beside an arched gateway with neon lights that spelled out Space Station: EARTH. The safety bar popped up, and guides wearing rubbery orange-and-green alien costumes helped the four scramble onto the platform.

"Warning," boomed the recorded voice as Joe pushed the exit door open. "You are entering uncharted territory—planet Earth. Good luck."

"Aye, aye, Captain," Frank quipped, holding the door for the others to step out into the bright California sunshine.

Nancy smiled at Frank, glad that she and Bess had decided to join the Hardys in Hollywood. When Frank had called to let her know that he and his brother were flying to Los Angeles to work on a case, she decided to spend some time with her old friends and get in some sightseeing. Fortunately, it wasn't hard to persuade Bess to join her. That very day they booked a flight and started packing summer clothes.

Walking out into the warm morning, Nancy was glad she'd worn denim shorts, a white T-shirt, and a beaded vest. She wasn't cold inside the air-conditioned exhibits, and she wasn't hot outside.

The exit of Space Race left them in a shady garden overlooking the back lot of Hollywood Gold Studios. The morning haze was burning off, revealing acres of neatly laid out buildings, walkways, ponds, and the facades of houses that formed tiny villages.

"From here it looks like HG Studios owns half of Hollywood," Nancy said.

Frank nodded. "The studio films most of its movies and television shows on that back lot in the valley below."

The upper level of the lot, built into the Hollywood Hills, featured the theme park, shows, shops, and concession stands.

Joe pulled a pair of reflector sunglasses from his shirt pocket and put them on. "Anybody want to ride Space Race again?"

"Later. There are dozens of other attractions to check out first. After we've tried everything once, we can go back to the rides we liked best," Frank suggested.

"What next?" Bess asked. She pulled the map of HG Studios Theme Park from the back pocket of her khaki shorts and spread it out.

They were gathered around Bess discussing a plan when a tall cowboy sauntered over to them. In his early twenties, he had auburn hair, warm brown eyes, and a big smile.

"Howdy, folks," he said, removing his Stetson to greet them.

Bess gave the cowboy a dazzling smile. Instinctively, she ran her fingers through her long, straw blond hair, arranging it so that it cascaded down her shoulders.

Watching her, Nancy smiled. Flirting was a way of life with Bess.

"You must be from the Outlaw West Show," Bess said, taking in his leather chaps and gun belt.

"Zeke's the name," he said, twirling a pistol on his finger, then shoving it into his holster. "Gunslinging's my game. Care to have your picture taken with one of the West's wildest?" He nodded to a dark-haired man who stood behind him, holding a camera.

"I'd love to!" Bess beamed, tucking her white V-neck T-shirt into her shorts.

Zeke stepped into the center of the group and dropped his arms over the girls' shoulders. "Smile, y'all," Zeke drawled. The photographer snapped the picture.

"Have a good day, folks," the cowboy said, winking at Bess. "'Specially you, miss."

"Bess is my name," she called after him.

"Pretty name, just like you." Zeke grinned, then headed off to scout new prospects.

"You can pick up the photo at the Camera Cave," the photographer told Nancy. He had a trim black mustache, sleepy brown eyes, and dark brown hair combed straight back. He had the weary manner of someone sick of his job as he handed her a receipt with his name—Orlando Nunez.

"Zeke won my heart," Bess said, dramatically clutching her hands to her chest. "Let's check out the ghost town."

"The Outlaw West Show doesn't start for another half hour," Frank said, pointing to the schedule on Bess's brochure.

"How about the Flaming Inferno?" Nancy suggested. "That exhibit opens in ten minutes."

"That was a great movie!" Joe nudged his brother's shoulder. "Remember the scene where the geologist descends into the volcano and falls, hanging only by a single rope?"

"How could I forget?" Frank said, putting his sunglasses on. "You must have rented that movie a dozen times."

"Look at you two," Nancy teased, eyeing the brothers. "Shades, tans, worn jeans, and baseball caps with the HG Studios logo. It didn't take you long to pick up the Hollywood style."

"Love ya, babe!" Joe quipped.

The girls laughed, but Frank just shook his head. "I find it hard to believe that we're actually in Hollywood to meet with the head of HG Studios this afternoon. Irwin Gold! He's a Hollywood legend."

5

"I wonder what he wants to see you about," Bess said, her blue eyes wide.

"He wasn't specific," Frank answered. "He just said that he needed our help, and HG Studios wouldn't have flown us in from the East Coast if it wasn't something important."

"It's so glamorous," Bess said. "Maybe he wants you to be bodyguards for one of HG Studios' top stars! Or maybe the studio is having trouble casting the parts of two adorable teen detectives! Or—"

"Or maybe all this sunshine is giving you heatstroke," Joe teased, feeling her forehead for a fever.

"Very funny." Bess batted his hand away with a playful swipe.

"I'd love to be there when he tells you why he called you," Nancy said wistfully. There was nothing she loved more than a new case to solve.

"You'll be the first to know when our meeting is over," Frank promised her.

"Okay, gang." Bess folded her map. "The Flaming Inferno is about to blow. Let's go."

Nancy heard the thundering noise before she spotted the mountainous spectacle. The facade of the Flaming Inferno resembled a rocky mountain with a glowing red cleft at the top. From hidden speakers came a loud, rumbling sound. "We're going *inside* that thing?" Nancy asked.

"This'll be great!" Joe stepped up the pace, then stumbled to a halt when he spotted the long line. "Whoa! Bad idea."

Frank sidled up to him and spoke quietly. "I don't like to pull rank, but we do have VIP passes," he said, fingering the plastic badge that was clipped to his black T-shirt.

"Right," Joe said, brightening. "Let me talk to the guide at the front of the line." Nancy, Bess, and Frank waited while Joe walked over to the wide, cavelike entrance. A moment later Joe whistled and motioned them to follow him.

He led them past the line and around the mountain to a door that was hidden from view. "The VIP entrance," he told the others as he held his badge up to the lens of a camera bolted beside the door. A moment later there was a buzzing sound, and the door clicked open.

"I could get used to VIP treatment," Bess quipped.

Inside they were greeted by a young woman in a khaki uniform with the name Heidi embroidered over the breast pocket. "Welcome to the Flaming Inferno. Since you folks have passes, you'll be the first through our exhibit today. Let's start off by getting you into the right mind-set," she said, stepping over to a rack of khaki garments.

"Don't tell me," Frank said, folding his arms. "You want us to pretend we're geologists, like Dr. What's-his-name."

"Dr. Hornsby," Heidi said. "I can tell at least one of you saw the movie." As she spoke, she sized up the group and handed each person a jacket. "These will make your journey easier. Because of the pyrotechnic devices used in the volcano, we keep the temperature low. It gets a little cool for many of our visitors."

The group slipped on the jackets and zipped them up.

"All suited up," Joe told the guide. "Any other instructions? Do you want us to monitor tremors or get temperature readings?"

Heidi laughed. "Just step that way—down the red tunnel—and enjoy yourselves."

Frank and Joe led the way down the passageway with rock walls resembling a cave. Lit by red floodlights, the walls seemed to glow with heat.

"The suspense is killing me," Nancy said as she and Bess followed the Hardys. "In the movie does Dr. Hornsby ever make it out of the volcano?"

Frank was just about to answer when a voice echoed through the tunnel, "But, Dr. Hornsby, no one has ever descended into the center of the Earth and survived."

A deeper voice answered, "Then I'll be the first!"

"That's from the soundtrack of the movie," Frank explained. "In the film the geologist meets ant people who live in the center of the Earth. He stays with them after he falls in love with an ant woman."

The tunnel opened into a shadowy, cavernous room of rock walls, spitting flames, and rumbling tremors.

Nancy paused in the entrance to study the high platform they would walk on. It zigzagged through the chamber, suspending visitors over what looked like rivers of molten lava. She noticed two fire extinguishers discreetly tucked in glass cabinets beside the entrance. They were the only reminders that this amazing volcano was simply a wonder of engineering and special effects.

"Check it out!" Bess said, leaning over the platform railing to watch the red-orange liquid bubble and churn below. "The lava looks so real. I wonder how they do it."

Frank started to speak, as a cloud of smoke shot out from the wall, completely enveloping him for a moment.

"Are you okay?" Nancy hurried toward him.

"It's just mist. Actually it feels great," Frank said, grinning.

A few feet ahead of Frank, Joe was watching colorful flames roll along the chamber wall, then explode with loud popping sounds.

"Volcanic fireworks!" Bess said, running ahead for a better view. The bright bursts of light played red and orange on her face as she stood beside Joe, gripping the rail.

"Better than the Fourth of July," Joe agreed.

Frank moved past them. The platform twisted to the left, and Frank paused in the bend as a cloud of mist shot up above him.

He was about to move on when he heard another popping sound. Glancing at the cavern wall, Frank stared at a wall of rumbling flames. This time, though, instead of rolling along the cave wall, the flames leapt out at the platform. Flames shot right at him.

Frank raced forward, trying to dodge the flames, but he was too late.

Twisting around, Frank saw that his jacket was enveloped in flames. He was on fire!

Chapter

Two

FOR A SPLIT SECOND Nancy froze in disbelief. This wasn't a real volcano. That wasn't real lava flowing under them, but the flames roiling over Frank's jacket were very real—and very hot.

"Drop and roll!" Joe ordered. Instinctively, he sprang ahead but was stopped by the flames shooting off the wall. How was he going to help his brother when Frank was caught on the other side of the fire?

Jolted into action, Nancy turned toward the entrance. "I'll get a fire extinguisher!"

"I'll get help!" Bess shouted, running behind Nancy.

Joe noticed that the blast of fire was subsiding. Taking a chance, he darted across the hot platform to where his brother was rolling on the ground. Joe tore off his own jacket and used it to snuff out the remaining hot spots.

"You can get up now," he told his brother. "Are you all right?"

"I think so." Frank sat up to peel off the charred jacket. "This thing took most of the heat, though my back feels hot."

"You scorched the back of your shirt," Joe said, watching as Frank lifted his T-shirt over his head. He touched Frank's back, which was a little red but not burned. "Looks okay to me. Lucky you didn't singe your hair, though."

"Really." Frank ran a hand through his thick, dark hair, then grabbed his cap and put it back on. "It could have been worse."

Just then the mist shot out overhead, and flames roared out over the platform behind them again.

"Much worse," Joe agreed, checking out the fire. The platform seemed to be fire-resistant, but with a blast like that anyone walking on it would be fried.

Something was malfunctioning inside the Flaming Inferno.

A few moments later Nancy returned with an extinguisher. Just as she lowered the canister to the platform, the lights flickered, then glowed white, and the flames throughout the exhibit sputtered and died out.

"They shut down the exhibit," Joe said, gazing into the pit below. The image of molten lava was gone now, as were the rumbling flames and mist.

Instead, the cavelike room was suddenly brown and barren.

"Someone switched on the emergency lights, too," Frank observed. Just then Bess appeared, racing along the platform with Heidi and another uniformed worker.

"Are you okay?" Heidi asked breathlessly. She examined Frank's back and shook her head at the charred jacket. "Do you want to see a doctor?"

"I'm all right," Frank reassured her. "What happened?"

"I can't apologize enough," Heidi said. "Normally, the flames don't even come close to the platform. Nothing like this has ever happened before."

"When I reached the main entrance, they were just about to send in a tour group of thirty-some people," Bess said. "It's a good thing *they* weren't the first ones through the exhibit this morning."

"It could have been disastrous," Nancy agreed, squeezing Frank's arm gently. "I'm glad you didn't get hurt."

Even though Ned Nickerson was the number one man in Nancy's life, she and Frank had always shared a special spark of attraction. She couldn't bear it if anything had happened to him.

"One of our park engineers is on his way here to check out the exhibit," the guide told them. "In the meantime it looks like we'll shut down for the day."

"I'd like to stick around until he gets here," Frank told her. Although he didn't know why Irwin Gold wanted to meet with them, he felt sure that

13

the head of Hollywood Gold Studios would want to know the details of what could have been a major catastrophe at his theme park.

"I'm sure Sam would like to talk with you," Heidi told the group. "He'll probably have a million questions about what happened."

Ten minutes later a tall, dark-haired, strikingly handsome man hurried into the chamber. He wore navy coveralls with the studio emblem on the breast, and he seemed to be in his midtwenties. "I came as soon as my beeper went off," he called out. As he walked, he was leafing through papers on a clipboard.

"Hey, Sam. Back from Japan already?" Heidi asked.

"It's been two weeks," he said. "If my parents had had their way, I'd be permanently vacationing in Japan. They didn't want to let me go."

Heidi nodded. "My parents live in Wisconsin, and they're the same way." Then she turned to Frank. "This is the visitor who almost got burned."

"Sam Tenaka," the engineer said, extending his hand. He had a brisk, no-nonsense demeanor.

Frank shook hands as he introduced himself. Then Sam introduced himself to the others, making eye contact with each one. "Sounds like you've had an interesting morning," he told them dryly. "And from this maintenance report, I can't give you any answers. Everything was on-line and working last night when Heidi and Clint closed down the exhibit."

"Who operates the fire and mist?" Nancy asked.

"They're worked by devices controlled by automatic timers," Sam answered. "Where was the fire that got you?"

Frank pointed to the exact spot on the rock wall of the chamber.

Sam studied the wall thoughtfully. "I'll have to check out the jets mounted there." Without another word, he jogged off along the suspended platform.

Curious to see how the flames were created, Frank and Nancy followed. Bess and Joe stayed behind to talk to the guides about the other park exhibits. Sam led them to a point where the platform gradually descended into an underground village of tiny houses with moss roofs and mushroom trees.

"This must be where the ant people live," Frank said.

"Right. But we get off here," Sam said, hopping over the platform rail to land on a catwalk.

Nancy and Frank followed him and then moved through two doors until they came to a balcony with a rocky surface that curved overhead like an awning. Glancing over the cement edge, Nancy realized she was looking out into the volcano room from a pocket inside the rock wall.

"Smart setup," Frank said, pausing beside her. "Looking down from the platform, you just see the overhang."

"Exactly," Sam called back. "And most of our equipment is mounted on this wall."

Sam went directly to a station on the balcony crowded with equipment. "The fire and mist that shot at you came from these jets," he said, pointing to two devices that resembled black guns. One of the jets was marked with red tape and a sign that read Warning! Hot Machinery!

"The problem seems to be that someone switched these two jets," he said, frowning. "Look at that! The jet attached to the gas line is pointing *at* the platform. The jet for the mist is pointing up in the air." He touched the steel mounts. "They should be mounted just the opposite."

"Could they have been switched by accident?" Nancy asked, although she had a sinking feeling the answer was no.

Sam shook his head. "We don't ever dismount these jets. It's just not part of the maintenance routine."

"But someone must be responsible for the safety on this exhibit," Frank pointed out.

"Let's see," Sam said. "Today is Monday, and the most recent safety check was done . . ." He leafed through the papers on the clipboard and whistled. "Ha! It was done by me just before I left on vacation. Everything checked out then. And the ride has been operating fine since then. Whoever tampered with these jets must have done it *after* the exhibit closed last night."

Nancy and Frank exchanged a knowing look. Something was definitely amiss at Hollywood Gold Theme Park.

By the time Nancy, Frank, and Sam returned to the volcano room, Heidi and the other guides had disappeared. Joe and Bess were talking to a slender woman in her midtwenties with wild red curls and a solemn expression. From the way she was dressed, in a chic navy suit, Nancy knew that the woman was not a park visitor.

"Hi, Sam," the woman said. "Thanks for calling me." Then she turned to Nancy and Frank. "I'm Sonia Gold, head of public relations for HG Studios."

"This is my brother, Frank," Joe said, "and our friend Nancy Drew."

"Are you any relation to Irwin Gold?" Nancy asked as she shook the woman's hand.

"He's my father," Sonia said quickly, then turned to Frank. "We're lucky that you came through this little incident unscathed. Your brother filled me in on everything—including your upcoming meeting with my father."

Before Frank could reply, Sonia rushed on.

"I'm so sorry about what happened, but relieved a little that you weren't an average park visitor. At least you knew how to handle yourself in a dangerous situation." She bit her lower lip, then added, "I won't have to worry about your talking to the media, will I?"

Whoa! Frank thought, somewhat put off by the woman's attitude. Don't worry that I almost got sautéed, just as long as the story doesn't give the park a bad name.

"You can trust us to keep things under wraps," Joe told the woman. Nancy and Bess nodded their agreement.

"Good," Sonia said, then turned to Sam. "Did you find out what went wrong?"

The engineer frowned. "It seems that our friend struck again. The gas jet was deliberately rigged to hurt someone."

"This *is* a problem," Sonia said tersely. "Well, Frank and Joe, we'll have to get you in to see my father immediately," Sonia said.

"But our meeting isn't scheduled until this afternoon," Frank pointed out. "We were going to grab some lunch, and—"

"We'll have some sandwiches brought in for you," Sonia insisted as she started walking toward the exit. "This matter is important enough for my father to juggle his schedule a bit." She paused to wave the Hardys on. "Let's go! I've got a cart waiting outside. We can ride to HG headquarters."

"Guess you girls are on your own for lunch," Joe said apologetically.

"Don't worry about us," Bess said. "We've got all of Hollywood at our fingertips."

"We'll meet you back at the hotel around five," Frank said. "We can have dinner together."

Nancy and Bess had booked a room at the Hollywood Grand, where the Hardys were staying. The high-rise hotel stood just outside the gates of the park.

"Great," Bess said. "See you then."

"Good luck," Nancy called after them, wishing again to be included in the meeting.

"Well," Sam said, tucking the clipboard under his arm, "if you'll excuse me, I've got work to do. I'd like to get the Flaming Inferno back on-line as soon as possible."

As he walked away, Nancy asked Bess, "What should we hit next?"

"I'd like to attend the taping of a TV show. Heidi told me we can get tickets from the information booth beside the Hollyrock Café."

"Let's go," Nancy agreed.

Within five minutes the girls were standing in line at the information booth. When Bess asked about tickets, the man in the booth punched his keyboard and stared at a computer screen.

"We've got plenty of seats for the Jane Lane talk show," he said. "And I've got two tickets for *Sunny-Side Up*. It's a comedy with—"

"It's absolutely my favorite show of all time!" Bess burst out before he could finish the sentence. "With Marla Devereaux and Tony Calavicci. He's so cute!"

"The taping starts at two." The attendant slid the tickets across the counter. "Enjoy!"

"You bet!" Bess said, scooping up the tickets as if they were gemstones. "Oh, Nancy! This is going to be wonderful. Should we head down to the studio?"

"We have more than two hours, Bess," Nancy reminded her. "How about some lunch first?"

"Oh—right." Bess turned to the glittering marquee of the Hollyrock Café. "Can you believe it? I was so excited I almost forgot about eating. But now that you mention it, I could go for a chicken caesar salad and a Twinkle soda. . . ."

Frank Hardy held on to his seat as the modified golf cart moved quickly along the service road that ran behind the exhibit buildings. Glancing back, Frank had to admit that the multimillion-dollar operation was impressive.

Just beyond the main park entrance, with its landscaped hill of flowers planted to spell out Hollywood Gold Studios, two modern buildings towered into the sky. One was the Hollywood Grand, where they were staying. The other was the corporate headquarters for HG Studios.

The driver pulled up in front of the building entrance, then leapt out to open the brass-and-glass doors. Sonia led the way across the lobby.

The elevator took them to the penthouse reception area, and Sonia went inside to speak with her father. A few minutes later she returned to usher the Hardys through the outer office, where Mr. Gold's secretary sat, and into the inner sanctum— Gold's posh office.

Three of the walls were floor-to-ceiling glass overlooking Hollywood—the colorful theme park, the long, flat rooftops of studios, and the curving route of palm tree–lined Sunset Boulevard at the bottom of the hillside. Near one glass wall was a massive slate desk set on a large Oriental rug. Sonia directed Joe and Frank over to a long, chrome-and-glass conference table. As Frank sank into a soft leather chair at the empty table, he wondered where Irwin Gold was. Then he heard a low voice coming from the high-backed chair behind the desk. The chair was facing away from the room, toward a glass wall.

When the chair spun around a diminutive man with hawklike eyes and a shiny head fringed with white hair was revealed. He said a few more words into his cellular phone, shut it off, then popped out of his chair.

"You must be Fenton Hardy's boys," the man said, setting the phone down on the glass conference table and shaking the boys' hands. "I'd know that devilish Hardy smile anywhere."

Seventeen-year-old Joe cracked a grin. Although there was some family resemblance, the brothers each had a distinctive look. Blond and athletic Joe had a lighthearted approach to life. His brother, Frank, was taller, dark-haired, a year older, and more serious than Joe.

"We're glad to meet you, sir," Frank said. "A little earlier I wasn't sure we'd make it."

Irwin Gold touched Frank's shoulder. "Yes, Sonia just filled me in on the details of your accident. Are you all right, son?" When Frank nodded, Gold took a seat and sighed. "I don't know what I would have done if something had happened to you. You're my last hope."

"So this wasn't the first mysterious accident at the park?" Frank probed.

"Mishaps like yours are the reason I've flown you out here," Irwin Gold answered, his dark eyes piercing. "Someone has been wreaking havoc at HG Studios Theme Park. There's a time bomb ticking away here—and when it goes off, we're in for a bloodbath."

Chapter

Three

So the fire in the Flaming Inferno was no accident, Frank thought. "You think that someone is causing these incidents?" he asked.

"I suspect sabotage," Irwin Gold answered, then snapped his fingers at his daughter. "Get Jason in here, and Ken Zubin, too." To the Hardys he explained, "Zubin is the head of security. And my son, Jason, is involved in the operation of the theme park. If my kids are going to inherit this business, I want them to know how it's run, inside and out."

While Sonia called on the intercom, Joe pressed the older man. "You mentioned other problems at the park. What were they?"

"Let's see." Mr. Gold sighed and leaned over to flip through a folder. "A family was slightly injured when their safety bars didn't lock on the Space Race ride. Our crew determined that two key pieces were missing on the locking mechanism."

Joe winced, knowing how wild that ride was. Without a safety bar, it could have been deadly.

"Next," Irwin continued, "our wardrobe department was vandalized. Someone broke in and slashed dozens of costumes." Irwin closed the folder. "And now that fire in the volcano."

"Have you reported these incidents to the police?" Frank asked.

The studio chief nodded as he slid the folder across the glass table to Joe. "They did the usual fingerprinting and questioning. But it's a big park, and they could spare us only two detectives. Their investigation hit a dead end, and our park security team isn't equipped to handle a secret investigation."

"We don't want security or the police creating a stir. Any mention of a crime wave at the park will scare off tourists," Sonia added.

"Have you considered closing the park until the troublemaker is caught?" Frank suggested.

Irwin Gold frowned as he shook his head. "For the past two years, the theme park has been Hollywood Gold Studios' biggest moneymaker. When *Western Hearts* flopped at the box office this year, we took a beating. We can't afford to close the park—not even for a week."

"But judging by what happened to Frank, it's clear that this saboteur means business," Joe pointed out. "How can you guard a huge operation like this against a killer? It'd be like finding a needle in a haystack."

"That's why I called you boys in," Mr. Gold said. "From what I've heard, you two can do the impossible."

Just then the door opened and two men entered, followed by a young woman in a white chef's uniform. She placed a platter of sandwiches on the center of the conference table, then wheeled in a cart with plates, utensils, salad, and drinks. Joe grinned at the sight. There was nothing like a hearty lunch to get his investigative wheels turning.

"Help yourselves," Mr. Gold said, gesturing toward the food. As Joe and Frank filled two plates with salad and sandwiches, Mr. Gold reached forward and plucked a roast beef sandwich from the platter.

As soon as everyone had served himself and settled in, Irwin Gold introduced his son. "Jason, meet Frank and Joe Hardy, the detectives I mentioned yesterday," Mr. Gold said as Frank shook hands with the young man who took a seat beside him. In a gray double-breasted suit, Jason was dressed for the part of a young Hollywood executive, Frank thought. His hawkish dark eyes and cool demeanor marked him as Irwin Gold's son.

"And this is our head of security, Ken Zubin," Irwin said, gesturing toward a short, stocky man with a brown crewcut. He seemed to be in his fifties and could have been an ex-marine.

The men shook hands, then Jason turned to his father. "Did we miss much?"

"We were just going over the problems at the park," Sonia answered.

Zubin rubbed his chin thoughtfully. "And did you explain the urgency of catching this lunatic?" he asked sharply.

Oh, great! Joe glanced over the reports Irwin had supplied. We have to find a needle in a haystack on a deadline.

"I was just getting to that," Irwin said. Crossing to the wall by the door, he pointed to a colorful poster with a collage of vampires, witches, zombies, and ghosts. The title *Haunted Holiday* was scrawled across the bottom. "This is our next film release *and* our next new exhibit."

"We're trying a new marketing idea. The theme park ride will open the same week as the movie. The film premieres tomorrow night. The ride opens on Saturday."

Joe stared at the poster. "Didn't I see a commercial for that ride last night on TV?" he asked. "It's supposed to be a voyage into the underworld of mummies and ghosts and stuff, right?"

"Exactly," Irwin said. "Jason is in charge of the Haunted Holiday ride."

"We've been advertising the ride extensively," Jason added. "We're expecting record crowds in the park when it opens on Saturday."

"A packed park with a saboteur on the loose?" Frank frowned. "Today's Monday. That gives us less than a week to crack this case."

"Do you think you can help us?" Irwin asked.

Joe and Frank nodded at each other, then Frank

said, "We'll give it our best shot. Do you have any ideas? Anyone with a grudge against you or the studio?"

Jason hesitated a moment, then answered, "There's one person I've been having trouble with. A screenwriter named Zoe Fortune—"

"She's small fry," Zubin interrupted, waving off the suggestion as if it were a pesky fly.

"But she *has* threatened us in writing," Jason argued. He opened a folder, picked up a few sheets of paper, and passed them to Frank. "These are copies of her letters. She's claiming that we stole the idea for *Haunted Holiday* from a script she wrote."

Frank quickly skimmed the letters. "'Give me credit, or you'll regret it.'" He read aloud from one letter. "'Pay the price or sacrifice.'"

"Do they all rhyme?" Joe asked. "Zoe Fortune must be a screenwriter *and* a poet."

Sonia rolled her eyes. "The woman is a poetic nightmare."

"Isn't this a matter for your lawyers to straighten out?" Frank asked.

"We're building a case against Ms. Fortune," Sonia answered. "But in the meantime, she's been harassing us with threatening notes."

"We'll check her out," Joe said.

Thinking ahead, Frank decided it would be best for him and Joe to keep a low profile. "Since we don't want to alert anyone to problems in the park, Joe and I will go undercover."

Joe nodded. "Can you line up jobs for us in the theme park?"

Irwin nodded.

"I'll work out the details," Sonia offered. "We can run you through the human resources office this afternoon and get you uniforms, badges, key cards —anything you need."

"And it would help if we had someone who could show us around the park," Frank added. "Someone who could check in with you periodically, if necessary. Joe and I won't want to attract attention by traipsing in here every day."

"Fine," Irwin agreed. He looked at Sonia, Jason, and Ken Zubin. "Any ideas?"

Before anyone could respond, Joe asked, "What about the engineer we met today? Sam Tenaka." Joe had liked his quick, easy manner. And since he'd been home vacationing in Japan for the past two weeks, it was unlikely that he was involved in the sabotage.

"Sam's a good man," Sonia agreed.

"That solves that," Irwin said. He pushed out from the table and snapped up his cellular phone. "Now let's all get to work."

The audience grew silent as the players stared at each other—the feisty waitress and the biker in the leather jacket and tight blue jeans.

"They make such a cute couple," Bess said.

Nancy nodded, not taking her eyes off the stage. She and Bess were in the fourth row—so close that Nancy felt as if she were in the diner with the actors.

"Why don't you forget this dump and ride off into the sunset with me?" the biker asked. He leaned back in the booth and stretched his long legs into the aisle, effectively blocking her path.

"And let your breakfast get cold?" she retorted, dumping a plate of eggs into his lap. The crowd roared with laughter as she added, "I'm sorry. Didn't you want those over easy?"

Overhead, the Applause sign flashed, signaling the end of the scene. The crowd cheered and clapped as crew members scrambled around the stage. Before the taping had started, the audience had been introduced to the cast and the director, Haley Gershen, who was now backstage in the sound booth.

The emcee, Stan Mossberg, whose job it was to keep up the enthusiasm level of the audience, popped to his feet and spoke to the audience on a cordless mike. "That was Marla Devereaux playing Brook, and Tony Calavicci as Slick, that irresistible biker."

The crowd cheered again as Marla stepped downstage and took a bow.

"Where's Tony?" Stan asked her.

"Costume change," she called back.

"Ah, that's right," Stan told the audience. "We'll be running this scene again, so Tony is going to need a clean pair of jeans since our property master, Izzy Kapowski, used genuine eggs in that scene. Hey, there's our prop man now."

Stan pointed to a short man with square black

glasses and frizzy red hair. He was wiping down the booth in the diner and seemed embarrassed that Stan was singling him out.

"How about a big hello for Izzy?" Stan proposed. "On the count of three . . ." He counted off and on cue the audience shouted, "Hi, Izzy!"

The man's face reddened as he nervously adjusted his glasses, waved at the audience, then slipped behind one of the walls.

"Isn't Stan great!" Bess said enthusiastically.

"Okay, folks, while we're waiting for Tony to change, let's play another round of questions and answers," Stan said cheerfully. "Ask me a question about the show, and I'll give you an autographed photo of Marla and Tony."

"I've read that Marla and Tony are dating off-camera," Bess told Nancy. "I wonder if it's true."

"Ask Stan," Nancy prodded her friend.

As Bess's hand shot up, Nancy noticed the man in front of them. He had turned around to listen to their conversation. Earlier he had asked Stan questions about Marla. What was her favorite color? Her favorite food? Her address? The man was obviously obsessed with Marla Devereaux.

Nancy had written him off as a devoted fan, but now she was beginning to wonder if she had misjudged him. He twisted around and stared at Bess. His cheeks were sunken, and his long dirty blond hair was slicked back in a ponytail.

"That stuff in the tabloids is a bunch of lies," he

30

told Bess. "I know because *I'm* Marla's boyfriend."

Surprised, Bess let her hand drop to her lap.

Nancy answered for her. "Is that right?" she said casually. "You must be—very proud of her success," she said, fishing for words.

His mouth twisted into a pout. "Yeah. But I hate to see her flirting with Calavicci. And I don't like to hear rumors about her from kids like you," he finished, glaring at Bess.

"Sorry," Bess told the stranger cautiously. "I didn't mean to upset you."

When he turned back to the stage, Nancy whispered to Bess, "Watch it!" The man gave Nancy the creeps; she had a strong hunch that he was more than a little mixed up.

"Is there anyone in the audience who can sing the *Sunny-Side Up* theme song for us?" Stan asked, and Bess's hand shot up again.

The emcee picked a freckle-faced little girl and asked her to come out into the aisle. As the blushing girl sang into the microphone, her braces flashing, Nancy tuned out the song and focused on the man in front of her. She overheard him tell the woman beside him that he and Marla were engaged. Engaged? Nancy knew he was lying, but that wasn't the point. It was his obsession that concerned her.

Then he leaned down to tie his shoe, and as his T-shirt pulled up, revealing the waistband of his jeans, Nancy spotted it—the butt of a dark brown gun.

"I'll be right back," she told Bess, who was engrossed in listening to Stan. Nancy scooted down the row to the main aisle. She had to warn the security team about the armed man, but she didn't want to provoke him.

Nancy went down to the front of the bleachers, where an usher guarded the access to the stage. "Don't panic," Nancy said firmly, "but the long-haired blond man wearing the blue T-shirt in the third row is carrying a gun, and he's been making some frightening comments about Marla Devereaux."

The young usher's face froze as she glanced at the man, then at Nancy. "Wait right here," she said.

Nancy remained standing in the aisle as the usher rushed off to tell the two men who were guarding the exit. Just then the houselights went down, and the crowd cheered wildly.

"Let's watch this scene one more time!" Stan announced.

"Quiet on the set!" shouted a woman wearing a headset.

Hurry! Nancy implored the usher silently. They had to remove that man before the show went on.

"Quiet, please!" the stage manager shouted. "In five, four, three, two . . ."

The cameras were rolling.

Everyone's attention was on the set, where Marla was wiping down tables and talking with the cook. It seemed to be going well. Then Nancy heard a murmur rise from the audience. A few people gasped as the blond man stood up and pushed past them.

The ushers standing in the back darted toward him, but they were too far away to stop him.

He was barreling down the aisle, his eyes focused on the object of his obsession—Marla Devereaux!

Chapter

Four

NANCY EDGED up the steps and onto the stage as if to get out of the man's way. She knew he outweighed her, but she had the advantage of surprise. The man took the stairs two at a time. As he lunged onto the stage, Nancy planted her legs in a karate stance. With precision, she landed a kick against the man's hips.

The man went flying across the stage and fell to the floor not far from the table where Marla was standing and watching them.

"Cut!" The director's voice sounded shrill over the intercom. "What's going on out there?" she cried as three men tackled the man and pinned him to the floor.

"He's got a gun in his waistband," Nancy told a

uniformed guard, who reached down and yanked the pistol out.

Meanwhile, the houselights went up, and Stan calmed the audience. He joked that this incident was staged, that the man had escaped from a nearby studio where they were taping a detective show.

Nancy was amazed at how quickly everyone worked to get things back to normal. The man was hoisted to his feet and escorted out. "The police will take care of him," the guard assured her. "Thanks for moving so fast."

"Can we clear the stage, please?" the stage manager barked.

Just as Nancy was about to return to her seat, someone grabbed her arm. She found herself staring into the clear blue eyes of Marla Devereaux.

"Why don't you stick around backstage?" Marla suggested. "I really appreciate what you did."

"Marla—we need you in the diner!" the stage manager shouted.

"In a second, Casey," Marla answered, then went back to Nancy. "I can't talk now. Can you spare me a minute after the taping?"

"We'd love that," Nancy said.

Marla instructed an usher to bring Nancy and Bess backstage. Then she ran to her spot, smiled, and called out, "Ready when you are."

"I can't believe this," Bess whispered to Nancy as the usher brought them behind the stage wall of the diner. She smiled at the man who played the cook. "You just saved the cast of *Sunny-Side Up* from an attacker. And we're going backstage to meet superstar Marla Devereaux."

"This *is* exciting," Nancy agreed, smiling.

"Exciting?" Bess said. "It's unreal. Pinch me— I'm dreaming!"

Nancy and Bess were given security badges and escorted to a small, glassed-in booth, which was used by the director to coordinate the show. The people in the booth were focusing intently on four monitors that showed the various camera shots.

Sitting behind a control panel, the director could communicate to the crew members, who were wired with headsets. Whenever she wanted to speak to the entire cast and audience, her voice was broadcast over speakers in the studio.

Between takes the girls were introduced to the show's producer, Quincy Albert, a stocky man with a full beard. He was the only person in the booth who seemed calm.

"So you're the young lady who spotted that kook in the audience," Quincy said, shaking Nancy's hand. "Good eye."

"Nancy has a talent for things like that," Bess said proudly. "She's a famous detective."

"Is that so?" Quincy acted interested. "We were lucky to have you in the audience today. Detectives from the Los Angeles Police Department are interviewing the man now. Thanks to you, no one was hurt." He smiled. "Now, if you'll excuse me, I've got work to do."

While Quincy kept a low profile throughout the

taping, the director's style was just the opposite. Haley Gershen was a wiry, blond bundle of energy. She barked out orders, called out shots, and let comments fly freely.

"Camera two, come in closer, please," Haley ordered. "And can we get someone from makeup to take the shine off Tony's nose?"

"Everyone works so hard," Bess whispered to Nancy. "When you're watching a show on TV, you don't realize all these people are working behind the scenes."

"I know," Nancy said. "I'm amazed at how quickly the show got back up after that incident," she added. "No one seemed to miss a beat."

Hearing her comment, Quincy Albert folded his arms over his wide girth and explained, "That's because studio time is money. With both cast and crew on the payroll, every minute costs. And even though we have a hit show on our hands, HG Studios keeps a tight cap on our budget."

Since each scene was taped two or three times, it took two hours to complete the entire thirty-minute sitcom. After the last scene was finished, everyone from the booth filed onstage. From the wings, Nancy and Bess watched the cast, director, and producer bow before the cheering audience. Then it was over.

"Hey, there!" Marla said brightly when she spotted Nancy and Bess. "I wanted to thank you for what you did, but I didn't even get your names."

"I'm Nancy Drew," Nancy said, smiling. "And this is my friend Bess Marvin."

"We're from the Midwest, and we're here on vacation," Bess explained, shaking Marla's hand. "And I'm so happy to meet you."

"Bess is a big fan," Nancy added.

"I appreciate that," Marla said. "You know, I'm from the Midwest, too. And though I came here two years ago, this Hollywood stuff is still new to me. I've wanted to be an actress since I was little, but I never imagined the problems that went along with it. L.A.'s fast lane is riddled with potholes," she teased.

The girls laughed at her joke, although Nancy sensed that there was an underlying grain of truth.

"Let's head back to my dressing room," Marla suggested. "It'll be more private there."

The girls followed Marla backstage, passing several studio guards. Nancy and Bess showed their badges, and Marla joked with the guards.

"Oh, Ms. Devereaux," one of the men called to her. "Mr. Steele was looking for you again. I told him you were busy."

"Thanks, Murph," Marla called as she waved over her shoulder. "That Sly doesn't give up."

Behind Marla, Bess nudged Nancy. "Do you mean Sly Steele—the actor?" Bess asked.

"The one and only. If he would just be this persistent with his career, he might actually get a decent role," Marla said, then laughed.

Nancy wasn't sure what Marla meant, but she was glad the actress was in a good mood. "You seem to be in great spirits, considering that close call on the set," Nancy said.

"You don't know the half of it," Marla said, sighing. "That nut has been stalking me for weeks."

"Stalking?" Bess's eyes were wide.

Marla nodded. "It's been awful. He calls and leaves horrible messages on my machine. Or else he sits in his van outside my apartment building. Once I could see him watching my windows through binoculars."

Bess shivered. "Totally creepy."

"Have you reported him to the police?" Nancy asked.

"Every time I've seen him," Marla answered. "But by the time the police arrive, he's gone. Detective Bolita thinks that he must have a police band radio, which would allow him to hear the unit being called to my address. Then he can take off just in time."

Nancy frowned. "What about tracing the calls?"

"The caller always uses a different pay phone," Marla answered. "He's pretty clever—but he revealed himself today."

"How long was this going on?" Nancy asked.

"More than three weeks," Marla said. "Recently, I've had this eerie feeling that he's been following me around town. That's why I'm so happy that he lunged at me in public."

"Now I understand," Nancy said. "This isn't the start of a case. It's the end of a nightmare."

"Exactly," Marla agreed. The girls entered a corporate-looking corridor. There the girls flashed their badges to another guard. "I made sure that security called Detective Bolita immediately. He should be upstairs, questioning the man. It'll be great to be done with this terrible phase in my life."

They passed a suite of offices and turned down a narrow hallway. Each door they passed had a sign with a star painted on it along with a placard showing the name of an actor.

"Here we are—my dressing room." Marla paused at the door to press her fingers against the star. "I'm still not used to this celebrity stuff. Nine months ago I was waiting tables."

As Marla walked into her dressing room, Bess pointed to a door across the hall and whispered to Nancy, "Look! There's Tony's dressing room."

Before Nancy could respond Marla let out a bone-chilling scream. "No-o-o-o!"

Nancy and Bess rushed into Marla's dressing room. The actress was quivering as she stared at the mirror over her dressing table.

Bare lightbulbs circled the mirror, illuminating the message that was scrawled in bloodred lipstick:

YOU'LL BE MINE—ALIVE OR DEAD!

Chapter

Five

M ARLA COVERED HER EYES with her hands. "I shouldn't let him get to me, but I can't help it. How did he get so close?"

While Bess rushed over to comfort Marla, Nancy did a quick check of the room to make sure that the person who'd written the threat wasn't still there. The small wardrobe closet was empty, as was the adjoining bathroom.

"There's no one here," Nancy said.

"I shouldn't be so scared," Marla said, taking a deep breath to calm herself. "I mean, now that the stalker has been caught, I'll be safe."

Nancy wasn't so sure. It was one thing for the man with the gun to get into the studio audience. Tickets to the taping were given out to the general public, but how did he get past security and into this private area?

Before she could ask Marla, there was a flurry of activity in the hallway, and Tony Calavicci and Quincy Albert rushed into the room.

"What's going on?" Quincy demanded.

"Are you okay?" Tony went to Marla's side and gently touched her shoulder.

"I'm all right. Just rattled by this," Marla said as she pointed to the message scrawled on the mirror. "The stalker must have sneaked in during the taping."

Tony glanced at the message, then hugged Marla close. "I don't like that at all."

"Me, neither," Quincy added. "But we'll discuss it in my office. Detective Bolita is waiting there, along with the head of studio P.R."

"Sonia Gold?" Bess asked. To Quincy's unasked question, she said, "We met Sonia this morning— in the theme park."

Before Bess inadvertently gave them too much information, Nancy cut in. "Bess and I would like to go talk with the detective," she told Quincy. "There are a few things about this case that puzzle me."

The producer scratched his beard for a second, then nodded. "I guess it wouldn't hurt to have another detective sit in on the meeting."

"A detective?" Marla seemed pleased. "No wonder you spotted that man in the audience." She took Tony's hand as they filed out of the dressing room. "Maybe my luck is changing."

"I hope so," Tony said, his dark eyes full of concern. "Let me know what happens," he called to the others.

As Nancy followed the group up the stairs, she thought about the chemistry between Marla and Tony. The rumors seemed to be right on the mark. Those two had stars in their eyes for each other. She glanced ahead at Bess, wondering if she would be devastated that gorgeous Tony Calavicci was spoken for.

Quincy's office was in a corner of the building overlooking a busy section of the studio lot. Nancy barely noticed the workers, forklifts, and carts that passed by outside as Quincy introduced the girls to Detective Thomas Bolita. The Los Angeles detective was a thin man with a fringe of white hair and clear, intelligent gray eyes.

"And this is Ken Zubin, head of security at HG Studios," Quincy added. A round, ruddy-faced man with a brown crewcut gave Nancy a strong handshake.

Haley Gershen, the show's director was also there, scribbling notes on her script. Nancy sensed that this woman was all business; she probably called out camera angles in her sleep!

"Nancy is the one who spotted the gun on your suspect," the producer explained.

"Good work, Nancy," Detective Bolita said, shaking her hand.

"Yes," Sonia agreed. "We're very grateful. This gives us a good reason to use metal detectors on the audiences. Any word on getting that system on-line?" she asked, turning to the head of security.

"That's an expensive proposition." Ken Zubin's cheeks puffed out as he frowned. "We're still looking into it."

Nancy eyed the man skeptically as she and Bess sat down at the conference table. After such a close call on the set, she would have expected the studio to be more responsive.

Sonia Gold extracted a sheet of paper from her leather folder and handed it to Quincy. "I've prepared this statement for you to read to the reporters outside. It says Marla was being stalked and that a suspect has been taken into custody on the *Sunny-Side* set. That should satisfy everyone."

"There's just one problem," said Detective Bolita. "Dwayne Tooley, the man who interrupted your taping, is not the stalker."

"What?" Sonia's jaw dropped as everyone turned to stare at the cop.

"How can you be so sure?" Marla's voice quavered as she tried to hold back her disappointment.

Bolita counted off the reasons on his fingers. "First, his rental car isn't a white minivan like the one you've seen outside your apartment. Number two, the man has been in town for just two days. A quick computer check confirmed his whereabouts before then. He was serving time in state prison for armed robbery."

"So he's on parole?" Zubin asked.

The detective nodded. "Which he's just violated

in a big way. You don't have to worry about Tooley. He'll be off the streets for a while."

"But if he's been in prison, he can't be the man who's been following me around," Marla said.

"And he probably didn't write that threat on your mirror," Nancy added. It was hard to believe, but Marla was being stalked by two separate people!

"What's this about a threat?" Bolita asked.

Nancy explained about the message they'd discovered in Marla's dressing room.

"This stinks," Haley said earnestly. "And how did Tooley get past security?"

All eyes were suddenly on Zubin, who stiffened in his chair and didn't respond.

"There's a good chance that he didn't," Nancy suggested. "Your backstage security seems pretty tight. The message may have come from the inside —from someone who works here."

"I'll have my people find out if anyone saw Tooley backstage," Zubin offered, "but the rules are tight. Nobody gets in without a pass."

"I have a hunch you're right," the detective told Nancy. "These past few weeks, I've been wondering how the stalker knew so much about Marla's schedule. It would make sense that it's someone who works here, who watches her all day long."

"How awful," Bess said.

"Marla, does anyone come to mind?" Nancy probed. "Someone who might be angry at you for some reason?"

Marla's blue eyes sparkled with tears as she tried to concentrate. She searched the concerned faces around her, then broke down and sobbed. "I—I'm sorry," she choked out, wiping the tears from her face. "I just don't know."

"This is the limit," Haley snapped. "We've been complaining about security for weeks. We've got to take care of our talent. Can we get some action now?"

"Nothing less than a personal bodyguard for Marla," Quincy insisted. "She needs protection around the clock."

"There's no money in the budget for that," Sonia reminded them.

"Besides, it would set a bad precedent, and it implies that our security force can't handle its job—which is *not* true," Zubin said firmly. "Let's not overreact here. If Marla gets a bodyguard, every actor on the lot will be demanding personal security. Do you know what that would cost?"

"But I thought that lots of actors had bodyguards," Bess said.

"Just superstars," Quincy explained. "And those guards are usually paid for by the actor."

"There's no way *I* can afford a bodyguard," Marla said, sniffling. Since this was her first major acting job, Nancy realized, her salary had to be modest.

"I'm sorry," Zubin said, holding up his beefy hands. "But a bodyguard is out of the question."

"This leaves me with nothing to tell the media,"

46

Sonia complained. "They're going to have a field day with us."

But the P.R. director's problems paled in comparison with Marla's dilemma. With her tear-stained face, the actress seemed so vulnerable. Nancy knew she had to do something. "Maybe Bess and I can help. I'd like a shot at nailing the man who's been stalking you. Since we'll be here for the next week or so, Bess and I could devote all our time to this case."

Marla's chin lifted hopefully. "Do you think you could stop him?"

"Nancy's solved hundreds of mysteries," Bess said proudly.

"I'd appreciate anything you can do," Marla said sincerely. "I don't know where else to turn."

"Nancy, let me remind you that this is a dangerous case," Detective Bolita added. "I'd hate to see you getting in over your head."

"I'll be careful," she promised. "And we'll keep you informed of our every step. I've worked with the police many times." Sensing that Bolita still had his doubts, she gave him the name of River Heights's police chief.

"I, for one, will sleep better tonight knowing that Nancy's on the case," Quincy said.

"Then it's settled," Haley said, snatching her script and standing up. "Now if you'll excuse me, I've got some things to take care of."

"In the meantime," added Zubin, "we'll keep our guards alert here at the studio."

"You've got the phone number for our hotline," Detective Bolita reminded Marla. "Don't hesitate to use it."

That night Nancy, Bess, Marla, and the Hardys had dinner at a restaurant overlooking the beach in Santa Monica. A breeze blew in off the ocean, but the terrace dining area was protected by a glass panel that blocked the wind. As they ate, they discussed Marla's problem.

"So by the end of the meeting, everyone agreed that Nancy would be perfect for the case," Bess said, finishing off the story. She reached for her Twinkle lemon soda.

"Now that you've checked out of the hotel, what's your plan?" Joe asked Nancy. He and Frank had helped Nancy and Bess load their suitcases in Nancy's rental car.

"For starters, either Bess or I will stick with Marla twenty-four hours a day," Nancy explained, smiling at the actress. "Tomorrow we'll shadow her at the studio," Nancy continued as she cut up the last few bites of her swordfish. "If the stalker works at the studio, he may slip up. I want to be there to catch him."

Since the Hardys hadn't volunteered any information about their meeting with the head of HG Studios, Nancy decided not to bring it up in front of Marla. Instead, she waited until after dinner, when they were walking along the Santa Monica Pier.

Bess and Marla wanted to ride the antique carousel with its painted horses and flashing mirrors, and Nancy decided Marla would be safe enough with Bess. She then motioned the guys out to the pier.

"So what's the scoop with Irwin Gold?" she asked, her eyes flashing excitedly.

"I'm glad you waited to ask," Frank said. "Since the case is so sensitive, we can't discuss it around anyone—not even Marla."

Frank and Joe told Nancy the details of their meeting with the Gold family. "So we're going undercover to find out who's trying to sabotage the theme park," Joe said.

"We start work tomorrow," Frank added. "I'll be working in the maintenance department, and Joe will be trained as a guide."

"I just wish I didn't have to wear that dorky uniform," Joe said. "It'll make me look like a walking banana."

Frank rolled his eyes. "When did you become fashion conscious?"

Two hours later Nancy parked her rental car on the street near where Marla lived, in the hills of West Hollywood.

"It's the top floor of the pink building," Marla said, pointing to a two-story stucco building set into the hill.

Ten minutes later the girls had lugged their suitcases up the pink cement staircase and into Marla's guest bedroom, which had twin beds covered with lilac floral comforters.

"It's small," Marla said, pulling up the shade on

the window between the beds. "But if you look out this corner, you can actually see the skyline of Los Angeles."

"It's fine," Bess said cheerfully. "I'm just surprised that you're so—normal. I thought that all TV stars lived in fancy mansions with guards, gates, servants, and big swimming pools."

"Some of us are still working our way to the top," Marla said with a grin.

Nancy pressed her nose to the glass. Sure enough, the lights of a handful of skyscrapers glowed on the other side of the hazy valley. Directly below them, Nancy could see their rental car.

"From this window, we should be able to see the stalker's van, right?" Nancy asked, turning to Marla.

"Right." Marla nodded, then took a deep breath as if to clear her mind of the subject. "Why don't you two get unpacked?" she suggested. "I'm going to call Tony."

As soon as Marla was out the door, Bess nudged Nancy. "The tabloids were right. Tony and Marla *are* an item. She told me all about it while we were riding the carousel."

"I sensed that when I saw them together," Nancy said.

"They make such a cute couple," Bess said.

Nancy was unzipping her garment bag when she heard the beep of Marla's answering machine. She must have turned it on to check her messages, Nancy thought.

"Marla, this is Sly."

"The ex-boyfriend," Bess added, her brows raised as she listened in.

"I know you've been avoiding me. Let's have lunch—just a friendly lunch. I'm getting sick of tracking you down. Call me."

Then the message clicked off, and Nancy made a mental note to ask Marla if she and Sly had parted on friendly terms.

The machine beeped again, and the next message was eerily quiet. Nancy was hanging a dress in the closet when she heard a raspy sound on the tape. Suddenly Nancy froze.

It was the sound of slow, heavy breathing, then a low, gravelly voice. That of the stalker? Nancy rushed out into the hall. Marla was standing rigid; the voice clearly unnerved her. As the chilling message played on, Nancy understood Marla's panic.

"How was your dinner, Marla? I saw you stab that swordfish. Would you like to swim with the fishes? Think about it. Because if I can't have you, no one will."

Chapter

Six

Is THAT HIM?" Nancy asked.

Marla nodded, her face pale with fear. She winced as the voice broke into diabolic laughter.

"The stalker?" Bess joined them in the hallway and paused to listen. "He sounds so . . . evil."

The tape went on with a second message, just as terrifying as the first, although the caller never spoke another word. There was just the raspy sound, like the sinister growl of a trapped animal, then the sickening sound of heavy breathing.

The stalker's messages were certainly effective. Nancy went to the window and peered down at the street, wondering if she and Marla and Bess would ever be able to get some sleep. "There's no one there," she said aloud. "But he must have trailed us to Santa Monica."

"He knows what I ate for dinner," Marla said, her voice cracking as she hugged herself. "He must have been watching our every move."

"It's scary," Bess agreed, biting her lip. "Especially since he knows where you live."

"And he has my phone number," Marla added, "even though it's unlisted and I've changed it twice in the last two months."

"He must have an inside connection," Nancy said, thinking aloud. "How about past boyfriends —like Sly? Did you two part on good terms?"

"It was a little rocky for a while," Marla admitted. "Sly was disgruntled when we broke up, and it only got worse when *Sunny-Side* became a hit."

"Was he jealous?" asked Bess.

"Yes," Marla said. "It didn't help that his career seemed to be on a down swing. He lost a big part in a movie and ended up as a guest on a soap opera. I felt like he was clinging to me just to stay in the limelight."

"Did you ever think that Sly might be the stalker?" Nancy asked.

"Sly?" Marla seemed shocked by the suggestion. "I never thought of it. But I suppose it's possible."

"And he was on the set today," Nancy recalled. "That guard mentioned he was looking for you. He could have left that message in your dressing room."

Marla gasped. "That's right!"

"With all the studio security, how can Sly get on the set so easily?" Bess asked.

"*Dawning Light,* the soap that Sly is guesting on, tapes in the studio next to ours," Marla explained. "He's a studio employee, and he's got an ID card to move around the compound."

Nancy frowned. "That's not a very safe system. HG Studios employs thousands of people. There has to be a way to make *Sunny-Side Up* a closed set—at least until the stalker is caught."

"That's Ken Zubin's job," Marla said.

"I'll talk to him about it in the morning," Nancy offered, though she wasn't looking forward to dealing with the disgruntled head of security. "Besides Sly, are there any other former boyfriends who might have a grudge?"

"Sly is the only one here in L.A."

"And before that?" Nancy pressed.

"My love life always took a backseat to acting. I dated while I was in acting school but no one serious."

"Any persistent fans?" Nancy asked. "Guys with major crushes?"

Marla thought for a moment, then snapped her fingers. "Izzy Kapowski—our prop master!"

"We saw him at the taping," Bess recalled.

"He's had a crush on me since we taped the pilot," Marla admitted. "At first I thought it was sweet, but then he started to bug me."

"He's worth checking out," Nancy said. "Now I've got a few leads to follow up in the morning."

"Which always comes too soon," Marla said, yawning. "I have a nine o'clock table reading. And this is a busy week, with the film premiere tomorrow night and an autographing on Wednesday. I'm going to call Tony, then dive into bed."

"Me, too," Bess said, then amended, "I mean, the part about jumping into bed. But tell Tony we said hi."

Long after the girls had slipped into bed and Bess was asleep, Nancy lay awake staring at the ceiling. It was hard to sleep, knowing that the stalker might drive up at any minute.

She threw back her covers and tiptoed over to the window. Outside the street was quiet, but for how long?

I wish he would show his face, she thought. Nancy had to admit that she didn't feel completely secure in Marla's apartment. She had checked all the locks on the doors and windows, and she knew the detective's number by heart. But anything could happen.

She felt as if they had set up a trap for the stalker—and *they* were the bait.

The stalker was a no-show that night.

Nancy's nerves were slightly on edge on Tuesday morning. It was gray and overcast. A milky haze clung over the valley as the girls drove up the winding hill to HG Studios.

"Typical L.A. weather," Marla said as she pulled her Bronco up to the guard booth on the studio lot. "The haze should burn off by noon."

After a quick ID check, the guard leaned out of the booth and handed Nancy and Bess badges. "You'll need to wear these while you're here."

"Thanks!" Marla pulled away from the booth, then turned toward the parking garage where each member of the cast and crew had his or her own parking spot. Marla braked at a stop sign, and a golf cart rolled past with a short blast of its horn. "Cowboys coming from the wardrobe department," Marla observed.

"Friends of yours?" Nancy asked, turning to see who was riding in the cart.

"Hey—no! It's a friend of mine!" Bess exclaimed, leaning out the window and waving. "Hi, Zeke! How's it going?"

Already dressed in his western garb, the actor was riding with a handful of other "gunslingers" toward the theme park. He stood up in the open vehicle and waved his Stetson at the girls. "Hey, Bess! When're you goin' to pay the Outlaw West a visit?"

"Soon!" she called to him. She watched as the cart disappeared behind a building, then turned back to the other girls. "He remembered me! Now I'm *definitely* going to see his show."

"Easy now, Miss Bess," Marla said with a slow drawl. "You don't want to go 'n' git your heart lassoed."

Bess blushed as she nudged Marla in the shoulder. "I'm a pushover for a handsome face."

Ten minutes later they were inside the cool studio where a huge table had been set up onstage. Actors and people from the crew milled around, laughing, talking, sipping coffee, and eating doughnuts from a snack table set up in front of the bleachers. Juan

Mendez, the actor who played the cook, had piled a plate high with half a dozen frosted pastries.

"Juan, where do you put it all?" Marla teased as she breezed past him on her way toward the stage.

"I got to keep up my strength," he insisted.

The atmosphere was much more relaxed than it had been the day before. Gone were the cameras and sound equipment. And since they would not be taping that day, the stage lights were dim. As the three girls walked onstage, Nancy glanced at the diner set. It looked like an abandoned restaurant.

"Hey, Marla!" a young woman called from the table. She had dark, almond-shaped eyes and shiny black hair that fell to her chin in a sleek cut. "We saved you a seat," she said, patting the folding chair between her and Tony.

"Right between my two favorite people," Marla said, resting her hands on Tony's shoulders as Bess and Nancy stood beside her. "I don't know if you guys all met yesterday. Nancy and Bess, this is Tony Calavicci, heartbreaker of our show. And this," she said, dropping a hand on the woman's shoulder, "is my good friend Chelsea Woo. She plays Squeak, the owner of the diner."

"I'm Nancy Drew, and this is Bess Marvin," Nancy said, shaking the actors' hands.

"We're so excited to meet you!" Bess said enthusiastically. "I love your show."

"Me, too," Tony said, tossing his dark hair out of his eyes. "It pays a lot of bills."

"Wise guy!" Marla nudged him as she dropped

into the chair beside him. "Nancy is here to help snag—my shadow," she said cryptically.

"Really?" Chelsea brightened. "Thank goodness. We've been so worried about Marla. I don't know how she's held up under the stress." She turned to Marla. "If I were in your shoes, I would've quit the show weeks ago."

"That's hardly a solution," Marla said.

"Besides," Tony teased, "what fun would the diner be without its sexiest waitress?"

Just then Chelsea jumped up from the table, her eyes on a man who'd just arrived on the set. "Excuse me," she said, then darted off. Nancy watched as she threw herself into the man's arms and gave him a big hug. Dressed in an elegant suit, he could have just stepped off the pages of a fashion magazine—dark eyes, curly brown hair, high cheekbones, and an arrogant expression.

The director went to the head of the table and dropped her script book there with a thud. "People, I need you to settle down. Let's start on time today—for once."

"You guys can have a seat in the audience," Marla told Nancy and Bess. "Only staff, writers, and talent are allowed to sit at the table."

As Nancy followed Bess to the bleachers, she recognized the producer, Quincy Albert, seated at the head of the table beside Haley. He motioned for Chelsea's friend to join him.

"Jason Gold will be sitting in today," Haley said, gesturing to the man in the expensive suit. "Be nice to him or he'll fire us all."

Laughter rumbled through the room, and Haley responded with a grin. "Just kidding. He's actually going to work on the show next season." She rolled her eyes. "I guess that means we're being picked up for next season?"

"I'll put in a good word with Dad," Jason said with a broad smile, and the group chuckled again.

"He must be Sonia Gold's brother," Nancy whispered to Bess. Although Sonia was a redhead and Jason had brown hair, Nancy could see the family resemblance. From the way Chelsea had greeted him, it appeared they were dating.

"And look who's lurking near Marla," Bess said, staring at the set, where the prop master was sitting on the counter of the diner. "It's Izzy Kapowski, the guy who has a crush on her."

Nancy followed her friend's line of vision to the man with frizzy red hair and big black glasses. Nancy noticed him glancing at Marla, and she felt a little sorry for him. The guy was obviously head over heels for Marla, but it was a lost cause. From the way Marla's face lit up whenever Tony was near, Nancy knew that the actress was crazy about Tony.

Izzy was the odd man out.

On the hillside above the HG Studios lot, Joe stood in the garden of the theme park and tried to concentrate on what Randi Jo Mullens was saying.

Unfortunately, he wasn't having much success.

First of all, she was too cute. With her long, honey blond hair, freckled nose, and wide smile, she scored high in the looks category. Besides, she had a sweet southern accent. And she talked a mile a minute—too fast, considering all the facts about the theme park that he was supposed to soak up on his first day as a park guide.

"Now most of the theme park is contained on this level, although we do have a few attractions—like our studio tour—down in the valley," Randi Jo chattered on as they gazed out over the warehouses and fake villages below. "Any questions so far?" she asked cheerfully.

"Just one." Joe tugged on the lapels of his yellow-and blue-striped uniform shirt. "Any chance of getting this uniform changed?"

On the other side of the garden, Frank was walking beside Sam Tenaka when he noticed his brother flirting with the blond guide. It was Joe's first morning on the job, and he'd already let a pretty face make him lose sight of the case!

"Is there a problem?" Sam asked, noticing Frank's expression.

"Just my lovestruck brother, and I'll deal with him later," Frank said, then turned his attention back to the tour Sam was giving him.

Sam had already shown Frank most of the rides in the park, and they were now headed for the Haunted Holiday exhibit. "Is this ride going to be ready to open on Saturday?"

"Since the order came from Irwin Gold himself, the answer had better be yes," Sam said as he hopped over a barricade that blocked the path to the new ride.

The facade of the exhibit resembled a haunted house twisted into the shape of a giant bat. The two attic lights glowed red like a pair of piercing eyes, and the front door was shaped like the fanged mouth of a vampire.

"Home sweet home," Frank said dryly.

Sam laughed as he opened the front door. Once inside he paused in the entryway. "This baby's not on-line yet," he explained. "It'll be a lot creepier with sound effects and moving parts. Like these guys. They'll swoop down to grab at visitors' hair."

"Cute," Frank said, staring up at the rows of fleshy trolls with long, rubbery fingers.

Sam paused on the platform and pointed to a series of cars lined up at the end of the track. Each car was shaped like a coffin. "The visitors will ride in those coffins. For now, we'll just walk along the tracks. Watch your step." The engineer turned on his flashlight and hopped from the platform to the track.

Frank followed, moving carefully. The tracks disappeared into a shadowed crypt, and Frank wished that his eyes would quickly adjust to the darkness. The only light came from Sam's flashlight and the watery sunshine that filtered in from the entrance.

Ahead of him, Sam was explaining things. "There's an emergency switch behind that mummy's sarcophagus," he said, aiming his flashlight at a corpse wrapped in moldering linen. "And we built a special exit over here." The beam of light danced over a flock of suspended wax bats and into the cave behind them. "The cave is an exit for anyone who's too squeamish."

"Pretty clever," Frank said. As Sam moved ahead, Frank checked out the creatures that surrounded him. Just walking through the nonmoving exhibit made the hair on the back of his neck tingle.

Sam was already gone from the crypt, exploring the next chamber, when Frank thought he heard a shuffling sound. He spun around, just in time to see a flicker of movement.

What *was* it?

His heart hammered in his chest as he studied the figures that had been behind him. There was a zombie—half skeleton, half tattered flesh. There was a vampire with its satin cape flung wide. And there was the hooded figure of the Grim Reaper—Death—with its scythe of destruction held high.

"I must be imagining things," Frank muttered. Just as he turned away, something moved again.

The Grim Reaper stepped to the edge of the platform and swung its deadly blade down toward Frank!

Chapter

Seven

"WHOA!" FRANK YELLED, stumbling backward as the scythe cut through the air.

"Ha!" Death grunted. "That'll teach you to mind your own business. Go work on some other ride. This one's not going to open Saturday. It's never going on-line!"

"What?" Why would the Grim Reaper care about the opening of a ride?

Because that's not the Grim Reaper, you idiot! The truth hit Frank with the impact of a mallet. In the bit of light that trickled in, he could make out the shape inside the dark, hooded caftan. It was that of a tall, big-boned woman. This Grim Reaper was real, all right. And so was the scythe in her hand.

Sam bounded back into the crypt, the beam of his flashlight bouncing wildly off the walls. "What happened?" he called, shining the light on the woman. "Who are you?"

As she raised her arms to shield her eyes from the light, the woman dropped the scythe and knocked off her hood, revealing beaded dreadlocks and a broad, dark face with high cheekbones. "Cut the light! What are you trying to do, blind me?"

"Is that any worse than trying to take my head off with this thing?" Frank retorted, reaching down to pick up the curved blade. "You could've killed me."

"No way!" she snapped. "It's a prop. Fake. Just like the promises made by HG Studios."

"Lady—" Patiently, Sam moved the flashlight so that it wasn't shining in her face. "You're not supposed to be in here. Leave now, or I'm going to have to call security."

"Ha!" she barked again. "I own this ride. Haunted Holiday is my creation, my life's work."

"Wait a second," Frank said. Hadn't the Golds mentioned a screenwriter who was suing the studio for stealing her screenplay? "You're a writer?"

"Zoe Fortune, author of *Haunted Holiday*— until the Golds scratched my name off the script."

"Ma'am, if you have a beef with the studio, you need to hire a lawyer," Sam said reasonably.

"Already done," she said. "We've filed our suit, but the studio keeps stalling. They think I'll back off—but they're wrong. I'm going to haunt Haunted Holiday until Irwin Gold gives me the credit I deserve."

"But, ma'am"—Sam strained to remain polite —"this area is off limits to the public. It's dangerous. You could get hurt."

"Then I could slap another lawsuit on your beloved studio," she retorted.

Frank examined the blade of the scythe. It was definitely a prop, but it could have done some damage. Zoe Fortune posed a threat to the theme park. "Don't you care that innocent people could get hurt by your actions?"

She waved off his question. "You can tell Irwin Gold I'll be back," she said, gathering her skirts around her as she headed toward the cave exit. "You tell him that I'm his worst nightmare."

With that, she was gone.

"Do you think she's the one?" Sam asked.

Frank shrugged. "It's hard to say. She could just be a writer who's taking her cause public. But she makes me nervous. You'd better talk to Mr. Gold about getting her barred from the park." In the meantime Frank decided, he would do some checking on his own.

Back on the studio lot, Nancy and Bess slipped away from the *Sunny-Side Up* rehearsals to talk with the producer. Since his office door was open, Nancy leaned in and knocked on the frame.

Quincy turned away from the scheduling board, where he'd been writing in some changes with a felt-tip marker. "Hey, Nancy—Bess." He smiled. "What can I do for you?"

"We need to check on your personnel," Nancy

explained. "Can we look through your files to see if anything seems out of the ordinary?"

The portly man rubbed his beard thoughtfully. "The files *are* confidential. . . ."

"We're just looking for details that relate to this case," Bess assured him.

"Profiles that might fit the stalker," Nancy said earnestly. "We'll exercise discretion."

"Since you're trying to help, I guess I can bend the rules this once," Quincy said. "I'll have my assistant help you."

"There's one more thing," Nancy added, and explained that she wanted to meet with Ken Zubin again.

"He's a tough guy to track down," Quincy admitted, "but I'll see if we can get through to him while you're sifting through the files, which we have to computerize one of these days."

The girls followed Quincy's assistant to a nearby office. The personnel records for *Sunny-Side Up* were stored in three drawers, filed alphabetically.

Bess started a general sorting through of the staff files while Nancy checked out Izzy Kapowski's file. Nancy's gaze was immediately drawn to a notation made by Izzy's previous boss, the producer of another HG Studios show called *Going Places*. Charges had been filed against Izzy by another actress.

"There's a note here about Izzy menacing an actress named Glory Winters," Nancy whispered.

"I've heard of her," Bess said. "She used to star in a sitcom."

"Listen to this review from Izzy's last boss," Nancy whispered, then read aloud from the file. "'Although Izzy is a reliable worker, with more than eight years of loyal service here at HG Studios, we believe he would be better off assigned to another show, away from Ms. Winters.'"

"So this isn't the first time Izzy has paid special attention to an actress," Bess said.

Nancy read on, adding, "Izzy drives a brown station wagon. So unless he's renting a white minivan, he's probably not our man." She did make a note of Izzy's license plate number.

Nancy took one last look at Izzy's file. The person to contact in case of emergency was Izzy's mother, Louise, who resided at the same address in Burbank. "Considering his work record and behavior toward Marla, why is Izzy still working on *Sunny-Side Up?*" she wondered aloud.

"Good question," Bess agreed.

The girls made quick work of the remaining stack of staff files. Bess had checked the type of car each person drove. "Half a dozen of them drive minivans, and I noted their names," Bess explained.

"Good," Nancy said, skimming over the list. "We can walk through the studio garage with Marla to see if any of the vehicles resemble the van driven by the stalker."

Nancy and Bess were just closing up the files when Quincy poked his head into the office.

"I've got Ken Zubin on the phone," Quincy said. "He can't do a meeting, but he's got a few minutes to talk right now."

"I'm coming," Nancy said, grabbing her notes.

"If we're finished here, I'll head back to rehearsal," Bess said. "Marla shouldn't be alone at lunch break."

"Good. Catch you downstairs," Nancy said, and followed Quincy into his office.

"Let me put Ken on the speakerphone." Quincy pressed a button, then sat down behind his desk.

"Hello, Mr. Zubin," Nancy said, taking a seat. "We need to talk about security on the *Sunny-Side* set." She explained how Sly Steele had visited backstage the day before, and both men agreed that Marla's ex-boyfriend might pose a threat.

"The problem is, he's doing a cameo on a soap that's taped on our lot," the head of security explained. "We can't ban him from the studio."

Nancy also pointed out that any of the thousands of studio employees could use their badges to gain access to the *Sunny-Side* studio. "Isn't there a way to make *Sunny-Side* a closed set?"

Quincy liked the idea. "Can we do it, Ken?"

"I hate to make an exception for one show," Zubin said hesitantly, but after a pause on the line he agreed. "Considering Ms. Devereaux's problem, I guess we should do it. I'll have a new system in place in the next day or so."

"That's great," Nancy said. "I was also wondering about Izzy Kapowski. Marla says he has a crush on her, and from his work records, I see that this isn't the first time he's been obsessed with an actress."

"I'm familiar with Izzy's history," Quincy admitted. Briefly, he explained the situation to the chief of security.

"Do you think he's the stalker, Ms. Drew?" Zubin asked. "And could you prove it?"

"No," Nancy admitted. "But can't you at least transfer him to another show?"

"Izzy's job is protected by a union, and he's been with HG Studios for over nine years," Quincy explained. "If we're going to take action against him, we have to have an airtight case."

"We can't fire every employee who expresses interest in an actress," Zubin said coldly.

Nancy understood the legal limitations. "I'll see what I can learn about Izzy," she told them.

After Zubin hung up, Quincy thanked Nancy for taking on Marla's case. "With you nearby, I won't worry about her attending the premiere tonight or tomorrow's autograph session at the theme park."

"I'm glad to help," Nancy told him, "though I wish we could catch the stalker *before* Marla makes those appearances."

"Let me know if there's anything else I can do," Quincy said, then Nancy left his office.

As Nancy went down the hall, she saw it was nearly noon, and the rehearsal was scheduled to break around this time. She decided to go directly to Marla's dressing room just in case she and Bess were already waiting there.

When Nancy reached the dressing room, she saw that the door was cracked open. Nancy rapped on it quickly, then poked her head in. "Marla—anybody here?"

She stepped inside. No one. "I guess they're still on the set," Nancy said, thinking aloud. Just as she turned back to the door, she heard a noise from the bathroom. Was someone in there? If it was Marla, why hadn't she answered?

Her senses on alert, Nancy edged toward the bathroom doorway. There was no one in sight, but the shower curtain was pulled closed over the stall, and as Nancy stared, it flickered slightly.

Through the white luminescent plastic, she could just make out the shape of someone. Nancy's heart was hammering in her chest.

Someone was hiding in the shower stall. Was it the stalker?

Chapter

Eight

Nancy was torn. Should she go for help and chance letting the person escape? Or should she just open the shower curtain? Her racing pulse reminded her of the danger.

Finally she made a choice. She planted her legs in a solid karate stance, reached forward, and abruptly ripped the curtain open.

"Ohh!" Chelsea Woo flinched in fear as she backed against the shower wall. "You scared the life out of me, Nancy!"

"I have to admit, I was a little scared myself," Nancy said as Chelsea got out of the shower stall. Both girls walked into the dressing room. "What were you doing in there?"

"I was just looking for my script," Chelsea explained. "I thought I left it here when I was talking with Marla earlier today."

Nancy paused to study the young woman. A leather shoulder bag was slung over her shoulder, and she was carrying a gray canvas sack that was zipped shut. "Let me get this straight," Nancy said. "You were looking for your script in the *shower?*"

"Well, no! Of c-course not," Chelsea stammered. "But when I heard your footsteps in the hall, I got nervous."

Footsteps in the hall? On wall-to-wall carpeting? Nancy thought Chelsea was lying but didn't say so.

"You probably think I'm a coward," Chelsea went on, flustered. "But with all the talk about the stalker, I didn't want to meet him face-to-face, so I hid in the bathroom."

"Well," Nancy said as she walked out to the hallway, "I'm glad I was the one who found you. If you'd sprung out of that shower in front of Marla, it would have really rattled her nerves."

"Catch you later," Chelsea said, then ducked into her own dressing room.

When Nancy caught up with Bess and Marla on the set, they were in upbeat moods.

"We had a great rehearsal this morning," Marla said. "Haley has given us an extra hour for lunch, which means we can eat anywhere you'd like."

"How about a café on Sunset Strip?" Bess suggested as they stepped outside the studio.

"Great idea!" Marla said. "I know an adorable outdoor place where we can sit under an umbrella and watch the whole world cruise by. And if we don't take too long to eat, we'll have time to hit Rodeo Drive."

"Where all the exclusive boutiques are," Bess said, nudging Nancy. "When Marla reminded me about the opening of *Haunted Holiday* tonight, I realized you and I don't have anything to wear."

"You're right," Nancy said. When she and Bess had packed for their trip to L.A., they hadn't expected to be attending a glitzy Hollywood premiere. "Let's have lunch," she said. "Then we'll see if there's time to shop."

The girls went to the studio garage and got into Marla's Bronco. Winding, hilly Sunset Strip was just minutes from the studio. They passed a man in a flowered shirt selling maps to the stars' homes just before Marla slowed to a crawl and pulled up in front of Café Salada.

A valet whisked the Bronco away, and the girls were seated at a wrought-iron table topped with an orange and yellow umbrella.

"Arm yourselves, ladies," Marla teased as she slipped on her sunglasses. "It's time to stargaze." From behind their shades, the girls eyed cruising convertibles, classic cars, and limousines.

"I can't believe that big stars like you think it's fun to check out celebrities," Bess told Marla as they eyed a carload of guys wearing UCLA T-shirts.

"Everybody's a tourist in LaLa Land," Marla said with a smile. "And cars seem to be the center of L.A. life. Sun roofs, ski racks, desert vehicles, and vanity plates—that's L.A."

"Check it out," Nancy said, nodding at a license plate that read MUZKBIZ.

"You should get a plate that says EYESPY," Bess said, nudging Nancy with her elbow.

Nancy and Marla both laughed. "That reminds me," Nancy said to Marla, and recapped her meeting with Quincy and Ken Zubin.

"It sounds as if you're making progress," Marla said. "It really scares me to think, though, that the stalker might be someone who works on *Sunny-Side Up.* I feel so—vulnerable."

"I almost forgot. On my way back from Quincy's office I stopped by your dressing room." Nancy told them how she'd discovered Chelsea Woo hiding in the shower.

"That's strange," Bess said.

"I don't know when she could have left her script there," Marla said, frowning.

"I thought it was suspicious," Nancy agreed. "And her explanation didn't ring true. Maybe I should press her for the real story."

"It's probably just a silly mixup," Marla insisted. "Chelsea has been completely supportive through everything. And it hasn't been easy for her. When *Sunny-Side* was first conceived, *she* was the star of the show. The network decided to change the focus when they noticed the chemistry between Tony and me. Chelsea's role was scaled down, but she's been great about it."

"Maybe she's not as generous as she seems," Nancy suggested. "Maybe she's harboring resentment toward you for stealing the show."

"Not Chelsea." Marla shook her head emphatically. "She's one of the sweetest people I know."

By the time the girls finished their chicken mandarin salads, they had spotted five celebrities and one hunk in a red sports car.

"I don't know if he's famous," Bess said, checking out the red car waiting at the traffic light, "but he sure is cute."

With more than an hour to spare, they drove down Sunset to Rodeo Drive, the Beverly Hills home of expensive restaurants and shops.

Bess read the signs out loud as they drove past. "With this selection," she said, "we're sure to find outfits."

"What do you think, Bess?" Marla asked when they reached the end of the shopping strip. "Something elegant? Or would you rather make a splash with a racier dress?"

"Everything is so gorgeous," Bess said. "Now that I've browsed, I'm more confused than ever."

"Maybe you should try on a few things," Nancy suggested. "Just try not to fall in love with anything until *after* you've seen the price tag!"

Frank Hardy hung up the phone and pushed back from the desk. This maintenance office—one of many, according to Sam—was a small, dingy room behind the Attack of the Killer Spiders exhibit. It did have a phone and a few local directories and suited Frank's needs.

He'd spent the past half hour on the phone with the Writers' Guild, who told him that Zoe Fortune had filed a claim against Hollywood Gold Studios. The guild was willing to arbitrate, but so far the studio had refused to cooperate.

He'd also talked with a local lawyer, a friend of his father. The attorney had done some checking for him, but it hadn't taken long to verify that Zoe Fortune had filed a suit against HG Studios. For what it was worth, the woman was legitimate, the attorney said. She had a real gripe. Frank knew she also had a temper. Could she be the person behind the accidents at the park?

While Frank sat in the cool maintenance office, Joe was baking outside in the afternoon sun.

It didn't help that he was wearing a spacesuit with a glass visor that attracted and magnified the sun's rays. He was supposed to be posing as an astronaut so that park visitors could have their pictures taken outside the Space Race exhibit. But right then he was sweating so much, he felt more like the Incredible Shrinking Man.

Orlando Nunez, the photographer who had snapped a picture of Nancy and Bess the day before, was a sour, sulking presence behind the camera. Good thing Randi Jo attracted business with her sweet-as-pie smile, Joe thought.

"Over here, Joe!" Randi Jo motioned him over to a middle-aged couple in matching shirts. Joe squeezed between the man and woman and placed his silver-gloved hands on their shoulders. "Say Space Race!" Randi Jo coaxed. The photo was snapped, and Randi Jo handed the man a receipt.

"You can pick this up at the Camera Cave before you leave the park."

"That's the last one," Orlando called. "I'm out of film. Let's get out of here."

"Finally!" Joe muttered, although he knew his helmet muffled everything he said.

"Let's go," Randi Jo said, taking his hand. "We need to drop these receipts off at the Camera Cave, then we'll get you back to wardrobe to change. You've been a great astronaut, Joe. Isn't it a blast?"

Yeah, a real blast, Joe thought as he waddled along the path.

When they reached the Camera Cave, Randi Jo led him into the back room and loosened the hinges of his helmet. Joe lifted it off, sighing as the cool air hit his face. "They need to ventilate these things," he said.

"Give me two minutes to square this stuff away with Orlando, then we're off," she said.

While Randi Jo was in the front room, Joe checked out the hundreds of photos on the walls. Although every shot was different, the subjects were all tourists and almost all were smiling.

Against the back wall, he found enlarged photos that were very different. One photo was of a rack of torn garments. Another was of a sad-faced boy standing beside a sign that said Closed for Maintenance.

Just then Randi Jo and Orlando returned.

"Ready to go?" she asked.

"Sure." Joe picked up his helmet and pointed it at the unusual photos. "What are those for?"

Orlando's face was stony as he replied, "They're nothing. In fact, you shouldn't be back here. Forget you saw them."

"But they were shot here at the park," Joe pointed out. "What are—"

"Can't you listen? I told you to mind your own business," Orlando snapped, his dark eyes narrowed with anger. "You smile for the tourists, and things'll be just fine."

What a grouch! Joe thought. He was still curious but didn't want to alienate the photographer on his first day.

"Come on," Randi Jo said. "I'll bet you can't wait to get out of that marshmallow suit." She paused for a moment and pulled off his silver gloves. "That's better." Squeezing his hand, she gave him a smile that made Joe's heart beat faster. And from the way her emerald green eyes sparkled, Joe knew she felt the same way. No doubt about it—Randi Jo Mullens had fallen for the Hardy charm.

Chapter

Nine

T HAT DRESS looks fabulous on you," Marla told Nancy, as she stood behind her and zipped up the blue lace bodice.

Nancy slipped on the fitted jacket, then fluffed the gathered skirt. Glancing in the mirror, she saw that the dress matched the blue of her eyes, and it fit perfectly. "We're exactly the same size," she told Marla. "Thanks for letting me borrow it."

"No problem," Marla said as she leaned into the mirror to adjust her red sequined bowtie. She was wearing an elegant tuxedo-style pantsuit in black-and-white silk.

"I can't believe you couldn't find anything you liked on Rodeo Drive," Bess said, her red silk rustling as she came into Marla's bedroom. When she had spotted the off-the-shoulder gown on sale, Bess had to have it.

"We were running out of time," Nancy reminded her. "Lucky for me Marla has excellent taste."

"And we're the same size," Marla added, standing next to Nancy in front of the mirror. "In fact, except for our hair color, we could be sisters. The same blue eyes, nose, and . . ."

The doorbell interrupted, and Nancy turned toward the hallway. "That must be the Hardys." The brothers had been invited to the premiere by Irwin Gold, who was concerned that the saboteur might appear at the event.

Bess patted her hair one last time, then followed. "I can't get rid of the butterflies in my stomach. Just think—I'm attending a Hollywood premiere at the famous Mann's Chinese Theater!"

After looking through the peephole, Nancy smiled and opened the door. "Am I seeing double?" she teased, nodding at the Hardys' matching tuxedos.

"How do you like these penguin suits?" Joe joked.

"You look very handsome," Marla commented as she joined them. "You guys are going to be fighting off autograph hounds before the night is over."

"Thanks," Frank said. "You three look pretty good, too." His eyes seemed to linger on Nancy for a moment. Then he turned to Marla and asked, "Did Nancy tell you why we're going along tonight?"

"Yes," Marla said. "And I won't breathe a word of it to anyone." Nancy and Frank had decided that it would be safe to fill Marla in on the details of the Hardys' case, as long as she knew it was a secret. "But I'll feel extra safe tonight—being with *three* detectives!" Marla teased.

Nancy gave Frank a dazzling smile as he held the door open for her. She had always thought he was good-looking, but dressed in a tuxedo he looked like a prince. She felt a little like a princess herself, except that the royal coach was a Bronco.

Marla double-locked her apartment door, and then the group walked downstairs to the street.

"Hope you guys don't mind taking my car," Marla said as they all got into the Bronco. "The studio offered me a limo, but I'd rather skip the hoopla."

"I don't mind—as long as it gets us there," Bess said, strapping herself into the backseat. "I admit, I'm a little surprised that you weren't planning to go with a date. Someone like—Tony Calavicci?"

Marla laughed as she started the engine. "Are you getting a scoop for *Hollywood Tonight?*" she teased. "We haven't gone public with our relationship yet."

"Oh! I love inside gossip," Bess said.

"Well, keep your ears open tonight," Marla advised. "You might overhear something juicy."

"We all have to watch for anything unusual," Nancy reminded them. "The stalker could be in the crowd tonight."

"Ditto for our case," Joe pointed out.

"This is so cool!" Bess beamed as the Bronco

turned onto congested Hollywood Boulevard. Her festive spirit was contagious.

The bright lights and bustling crowds *were* exciting, Nancy thought. From blocks away, searchlights bounced into the sky. Store signs and movie house marquees glittered in the night as Marla steered the Bronco into the slow-moving lane of limousines pulling up in front of Mann's Chinese Theater. The height of their vehicle allowed them to see above the rest of the traffic and get a glimpse of the spectacle ahead.

A crowd pressed against the velvet ropes in front of Mann's, and strobes flashed as photographers shot one celebrity after another. An emcee stood at the edge of the red carpet and announced the arriving celebrities as they stepped out of their limousines. "Here's Hollywood legend and star of *Haunted Holiday,* Rod Magnum," the emcee said.

"Rod Magnum!" Bess leaned over the front seat to get a better look. "Oh, my gosh! He's so tall! And so—so real!"

"You may even get a chance to talk with him inside the theater," Marla said lightly.

"Oh, I'd die!" Bess exclaimed.

"And let's give a warm welcome to Lila Paige, Rod's costar in this captivating film," the emcee announced.

"Lila Paige?" Bess gasped. "I wish this traffic would move faster."

At last the Bronco crept up to the front of the theater, and Nancy could glance over at the line of fat red pillars topped by Chinese pagodas.

When they pulled up beside the red carpet, valets in white jackets helped everyone out. Then the emcee announced, "Ladies and gentlemen, HG Studios is proud to present the star of the hit TV comedy *Sunny-Side Up,* the lovely and talented Ms. Marla Devereaux!"

Marla strode forward, blowing kisses to fans in the crowd and smiling for the paparazzi. Nancy and Bess followed her, and as they walked up the red carpet Bess soaked up the attention.

"I could get used to this!" Bess said, waving at the audience.

"It is fun," Nancy agreed, glancing over her shoulder for the Hardys. They were hanging back, off to one side of the red carpet. She remembered that they were supposed to be undercover. It wouldn't be smart for them to appear on camera or make a grand entrance.

When they reached the theater entrance, Marla posed one last time, and then the photographers raced back to the curb to catch the next arrival.

Inside the spacious lobby other reporters were hounding celebrities. Nancy noticed the bright lights of a video camera shining on a gorgeous guy with one lock of black hair falling sexily over his forehead. It was Tony Calavicci.

The minute he spotted Marla, he waved her over. "It's my talented costar! Help me out over here, Marla. I'm drowning in questions."

Graciously, Marla joined him, and Nancy and Bess gathered around. Nancy recognized the interviewer, Liza Jenson from *Hollywood Tonight.*

"Any truth to the rumor that the chemistry between you two is more than just acting?"

Tony and Marla pretended to be baffled.

"We have chemistry?" Marla quipped.

"I failed chemistry in school," Tony said.

Outside Frank and Joe stood off to the side of the crowd amid security guards who were unobtrusively dressed in tuxedos.

Frank's eyes were focused on a placard that bounced over the heads of the crowd. On the sign was printed HOLLYWOOD HOAX! I'VE BEEN ROBBED! He could just make out the face of the sign holder—high cheekbones, smooth brown skin, and beaded black hair.

"Zoe Fortune," he muttered.

"She's *here?*" Joe asked. His brother had told him all about the woman who'd attacked him with a scythe. Frank pointed out her sign, and Joe whistled under his breath.

"Not too subtle, is she?" Joe said. He pointed at the pack of photographers. "And check it out—the photographer from the theme park, Orlando, is using a lot of film on her."

Frank was able to pick out Orlando Nunez, who was snapping one picture after another of Zoe Fortune. "What's he doing here?" Frank muttered. "And why is he so interested in Ms. Fortune?"

"The guy must free-lance at night," Joe said.

Free-lance? Frank wondered. Or was he getting paid by Zoe Fortune to have her photo splashed across the covers of the tabloids? Frank was distracted then by the announcement that the Gold family had arrived.

Amid polite applause, Irwin, Sonia, and Jason Gold emerged from their limousine and marched up the red carpet. Rising to the occasion, Irwin grabbed the emcee's mike and launched into a speech. "We at Hollywood Gold Studios are proud to bring you the best in entertainment—"

"Liar! Thief! Cause of my grief!" Zoe called from the crowd. Her cries were barely heard above Irwin's amplified voice, but Frank could see that she could easily turn this into a publicity nightmare. Two handfuls of eager photographers and reporters followed Orlando's lead and lunged toward the protesting screenwriter. Zoe was making herself heard, all right.

In the lobby Bess had run off to get Rod Magnum's autograph. Tony had been ushered into the theater, leaving Marla to contend with a camera crew from the show called *Girl Talk*. Nancy was watching the interview when the Golds entered the lobby.

While Irwin spoke with a reporter, Nancy said hello to Sonia, who introduced her to Jason.

"And where's Chelsea tonight?" Nancy asked.

"She— I need to maintain the family image," Jason said stiffly. "Dating an actress isn't really— people might get the wrong idea."

"What he means is that our father doesn't approve of his girlfriend," Sonia snapped.

"That has nothing to do with Chelsea," Jason retorted. "Dad just doesn't want the press to—"

"And you don't have the guts to challenge him," Sonia added, cutting him off.

"As if you do!" he retorted.

Nancy was sure that a family feud was about to erupt, but right at that moment Irwin Gold called his son and daughter over.

They're like trained seals, Nancy thought, watching them follow their father into the theater.

Across the lobby, she saw Bess chatting with Rod Magnum. Bess must be in her glory, Nancy thought as she turned back toward Marla.

A young man with sandy brown hair tied back in a ponytail had elbowed his way into Marla's light. Judging from the way he kept slipping an arm around her waist, Nancy had a feeling it was Sly Steele. When she heard him tell the interviewer about *Dawning Light,* she knew she'd guessed right.

"We've been so busy," Sly told the interviewer, "we haven't seen much of each other lately. But that's going to change, right, Marla?" He pulled her close for the camera.

"Sly is—a good friend," Marla said awkwardly.

"I'll tell you right here and now," Sly said with a smile, "I'm not going to let this woman get away." He stared at the camera, determination expressed on his face. "And what Sly wants, Sly gets."

Not if I can help it, Nancy thought, crossing her arms. Marla's ex-boyfriend was definitely someone to watch out for.

Nancy was glad to learn that there was assigned seating inside the theater. They'd be able to shake free of Sly during the film. He was one row in front of them and off to the left.

"He's the best thing that ever happened to *Dawning Light,*" Bess said as the lights went down and the opening credits began to roll.

Frank and Joe were ushered into the seats beside Nancy, and they all settled in for *Haunted Holiday.* The film was a spoof of horror movies, and by the end it managed to dredge up more underworld creatures than Nancy had ever imagined.

While the closing credits flashed on the screen, the audience applauded loudly.

"Looks like HG Studios has a hit on its hands," Frank said. He hoped the Haunted Holiday ride would open to the same success.

"There's a party at a place called Hugo's," Bess said. "Rod Magnum asked if I was going."

"It's on the invitation," Joe said. "Want to check it out?"

"What do you think?" Nancy asked Marla. She knew the actress wasn't interested in Hollywood glitter and glitz, but it was clear that Bess had her heart set on going.

"Let's go for it," Marla said.

Outside the theater, most celebrities had to wait for their limos to file by, but Marla's Bronco was fetched from a nearby parking lot by one of the speedy attendants.

Marla climbed into the driver's seat, and Nancy climbed in beside her while Bess, Frank, and Joe strapped themselves into the backseat.

"You'll like Hugo's," Marla told them as she

turned off Hollywood Boulevard. "But let's try to avoid getting a table near Sly. He's getting on my nerves."

"He *is* persistent," Nancy observed. As Marla turned the corner, something rattled under Nancy's seat. She glanced down, wondering what was rolling around on the floor.

Then something slid past her leg.

"What was that?" Bess asked from the back.

Instinctively, Nancy pulled her legs onto the seat as the object below her began to take shape before her eyes. It slithered under the dashboard, then circled into a coil.

"It's a snake!" Nancy gasped. The snake's tail made an unmistakable sound. "A—a rattlesnake!"

Chapter

Ten

"Eeeeooow!" Marla's knuckles turned white as she gripped the steering wheel in horror.

"Pull over!" Frank shouted from the backseat.

Nancy remained crouched on the seat, trying to keep some distance between herself and the snake as Marla slowed the car and pulled over to the side of the road.

"Everybody out!" Joe shouted. There was a clicking of seat belts being unbuckled, and the back doors of the Bronco flew open. Joe yanked Marla's door open and helped her out.

In one motion, Nancy unlatched the door and kicked it open. The agitated snake was still rattling when she slid out the door. Frank was standing beside her.

"You okay?" he asked, gripping her around the waist to steady her.

"Fine," she said. "But that snake wasn't too happy to be cruising in a car with five people."

From behind the open passenger door, Frank peered into the front seat of the car. "We've got to get that sucker out."

"This might work!" Joe said, holding up a tire iron from the back hatch.

Everyone stood back as Joe approached the open passenger door with the tire iron.

"Careful," Bess warned him.

Joe held the end of the iron rod, extending it away from his body as he reached into the car. His first poke at the snake evoked another rattle. Joe backed off for a second, wiped his forehead with the back of his hand, then tried again.

This time, he managed to hook the iron under the snake. With one motion, he swept the snake out of the car and dropped it to the ground. They were in a deserted area at the edge of a ravine designed to channel rainwater off the road. The five of them watched as the snake slithered sideways down the slope into the dry ravine.

"That was close," Marla said, still wide-eyed with shock.

Bess shivered and rubbed her arms. "How did that snake get into your car?" she asked.

"Someone must have planted it," Frank said.

"Probably the stalker," Nancy said. "We'd better drive back to Mann's and find out if any of the valets saw anyone tampering with your car."

"But first—" Frank said, holding out an arm to block the door of the Bronco, "let's check the car to make sure there are no more surprises."

Once they were sure the Bronco was safe, they climbed in. Marla was still a little shaky, so Frank took the wheel and drove back toward Hollywood Boulevard.

"This is awful," Marla lamented. "It was bad enough when the stalker was harassing me. Now he's trying to hurt me."

The valets were still in front of the theater, helping celebrities into their limousines. While the others waited in the Bronco, Nancy and Frank went over to speak to the attendants. "We're with Marla Devereaux," Nancy said, gesturing at the metallic blue Bronco. "You parked her car during the movie."

One of the attendants, a slight man with bright eyes and a thin mustache, nodded. "Yes, I remember putting it in the lot."

"Did you see anyone hanging around her car while it was parked?" Nancy asked.

The attendant spoke to another valet in rapid Spanish. Nancy, who spoke Spanish, knew that the answer was no.

"We didn't notice anything," the man said, "but we don't stay with every car. Sorry, miss."

Nancy and Frank returned to the Bronco. "No one saw anything," Nancy told the others.

"Too bad we couldn't dust the rattler for prints,"

Joe said as Frank put the car into gear and headed down the boulevard.

Hugo's was a sprawling mansion built into the hills of Laurel Canyon. Once the home of famous stars of stage and screen, it had been turned into a club for private parties. From the driveway lined with palm trees to the expansive rooms that glittered with chandeliers and shiny Mexican tiles, the place was legendary.

Since Marla was still shaken by the snake incident, the group decided to make a quick sweep through the jammed ballroom and find a table on the back terrace. It wasn't easy getting Bess past the stars, but once the group made it outside, everyone was relieved to escape the noise and heat of the crowd.

"Are you okay?" Nancy asked Marla as they settled in around a table beside the glimmering turquoise pool.

"I've had better days." Pushing her dark bangs off her forehead, Marla said, "I have to admit, this stalker is getting to me."

"I don't blame you," Bess said. "It feels as if he's everywhere." A shiver ran through her.

"Well, at least we're beginning to arm ourselves with information," Nancy said. "First thing tomorrow, I want to walk through the parking area for *Sunny-Side Up* to see if any of the cars match the one driven by the stalker."

"Good idea," Marla admitted.

"Besides," Nancy added, "we've made some

progress with security. Ken Zubin told me he's going to close the set to outsiders, which will help with guys like Sly Steele."

"I don't think Sly would hurt me," Marla said thoughtfully. "He's just—pushy."

"Very pushy," Nancy agreed quietly.

"Don't forget Izzy Kapowski," Bess told the Hardys. "Nancy and I learned that he has a history of harassing starlets."

Joe whistled through his teeth. "Sounds like quite a case, Nan. I hope something breaks for you soon."

"So far, *we've* only got one suspect in our case," Frank said. "And though I know Zoe Fortune has a grudge against HG Studios, I don't know if she's sabotaging the park." He told them what he'd discovered about the writer.

"Wow," Bess said. "She must have been mad when her movie premiered tonight—and she didn't even get to go in and watch it."

"If it *is* her film," Joe reminded her. "It's possible that another writer came up with the same idea at the same time."

"Well, we're trying to get her banned from the theme park, which might solve our case, one-two-three," Frank said, snapping his fingers.

"So fast?" Bess asked. "And Nancy and I haven't even had a chance to finish going through the theme park yet."

"Try it in a uniform that resembles a neon banana," Joe said. "Gross."

"Admit it—that uniform opened a lot of doors for you," Frank pressed.

"True," Joe agreed. "If I hadn't gone undercover, I would never have gotten so close to Randi Jo—or Orlando. Now, there's a guy who's involved in something strange."

"What do you mean?" Marla asked.

Joe told the group about the photos he'd discovered in the back room of the Camera Cave. "You know, those photos fit a pattern. The torn clothes were probably damaged costumes. The sign in front of the closed exhibit was probably taken the day the Flaming Inferno was shut down."

"Wait a second," Frank said. "Do you think Orlando is sick enough to slash costumes and rig the fire jets just for a photo opportunity?"

Joe shrugged. "Maybe."

"Or maybe he's planning to use the photos to blackmail HG Studios," Nancy said, thinking aloud. "They'd pay big money to keep that stuff from slipping into the hands of reporters."

"On the other hand, it might just be part of his job," Marla pointed out. "Maybe he's been asked to take pictures that the park can submit to the insurance company."

"That's possible, too," Joe admitted. "But whatever the reason, Orlando didn't want me to know anything about it." And neither did Randi Jo, he thought. Why were they so evasive?

B-r-r-ing!

Nancy pressed the pillow against her ear and

tried to block out the noise. Tired after a long day, she'd fallen into a deep sleep. As her eyes adjusted to the darkness, she tried to remember where she was.

Suddenly the room came into focus. She was at Marla's apartment. Bess was asleep in the bed across the room. It was the middle of the night, and the phone was ringing.

Nancy leapt out of bed and went into the hall just as the answering machine kicked on and a deep, raspy voice growled onto the tape.

"Marla—you looked lovely in that silk tuxedo. Sorry we couldn't attend the premiere together, but I sent you a gift instead. A sleek, deadly gift—with a cute little rattle."

Chapter

Eleven

THE STALKER'S VOICE jarred Nancy into action. She pressed the button on the machine to identify the caller, and a seven-digit number flashed.

"It's the stalker," Nancy said as Marla rushed into the hall. "Call the police and let them know. Maybe they can send a squad car to this number and catch him."

Bess appeared in the doorway just then. "I think the stalker is outside," she said.

"What?" Nancy and Marla said in unison.

"I woke up when I heard all the noise, and I don't know why, but I looked out the window. There's a van down there," Bess said.

Nancy and Marla raced to the window in the guest room. There it was—a light-colored minivan.

"It's him," Marla said. "But I don't get it. How could he call and be here at the same time?"

"Maybe he's using a cellular phone—or maybe he has an accomplice," Nancy said, moving toward the closet. She pulled a sweatsuit on over her nightshirt and slipped on her running shoes. "Make that call to the police *now*. I'm going outside to check him out."

"You can't!" Marla insisted, her eyes wide with fear. "He could hurt you if—"

"I'm not going to confront him," Nancy assured her. "But I want to get a closer look at his face—and the van. If I move fast, I might be able to get his license plate number."

While Bess rushed to the phone, Nancy tucked her hair under the hood of her sweatshirt and headed toward the apartment door. Marla pointed the way to the back entrance of the building.

Nancy cut around the side of the pink stucco building, taking care to stay hidden behind the row of green hedges. A sliver of moon was masked by hazy clouds, but in the dim light she could see that the van was made by Chrysler.

Peering through the hedge, she tried to make out the driver's features. Unfortunately, the shadowed interior, along with the glare from the streetlight on the side windows, made it difficult to see. The only thing she could make out for sure was a dark wool cap pulled low over his forehead.

Staying down, Nancy crept to the rear of the van to get the license plate number. But there were no numbers to read. The license plate was covered with a brown paper bag!

Just then the van's engine roared to life. Nancy was still kneeling on the grass when it pulled away from the curb and took off.

When the minivan was out of sight, Nancy stood up. She had gotten the make of the van, but would that be of any help? Frustrated, Nancy was heading back inside when a police cruiser pulled up.

"Are you the young lady who called in a complaint?" asked a uniformed officer.

Nancy explained that the stalker had just left. The two officers put out a description of the vehicle over the radio, then followed Nancy up to the apartment to fill out a report. "Our squad cars in this area will be on the lookout for that vehicle," one officer said, jotting down the information. "It helps that you got the make of the car, but we really need the license plate number in order to trace the owner."

Back inside, Nancy went to the door when the bell rang. Through the peephole she saw the solemn face of Detective Bolita. "I heard the description of the van over the air," he said as he followed Nancy inside. "Our perp got away?"

"Unfortunately," Marla said. "And he's kept us busy tonight."

"That's for sure," one of the officers agreed, and the detective looked over the man's shoulder at the report on his clipboard.

"Any news on where the stalker called from?" Nancy asked.

"From a phone booth on Sunset and La Brea," Bolita said. "And he's got a new trick."

"What do you mean?" Nancy asked.

"After we traced the call there, our detectives went to the booth and found a small tape player hooked up to the phone." The detective rolled his eyes. "Crafty, huh?"

Marla shivered. "What kind of a person would go to so much trouble to frighten me?"

A tense silence filled the room. No one wanted to answer Marla's question with the truth: she was being stalked by a man who was mentally off balance, maybe even psychotic. There was no telling what he would do next.

Marla played back the stalker's phone threat for Detective Bolita and the two officers, who had joined them. Then Nancy told the detective about the rattlesnake that had been planted in Marla's car.

"This guy's getting too close," Bolita told Marla. "For the next few days, you'd be safer staying with a friend—or at a hotel with a security force. It would throw the stalker off, and maybe buy us some time."

"I'll think about it," Marla said reluctantly.

She seemed so worn down, Nancy thought. Marla's skin was pale, and she had dark circles under her eyes.

After the police left, Marla was too upset to sleep. She curled up on the living room sofa under a blanket, aimlessly switching TV channels with the remote control.

"Want some company?" Nancy offered, and Bess nodded in agreement.

Marla shook her head. "I just need to unwind. I'll see you guys in the morning."

Crawling under the covers, Nancy felt discouraged by her lack of progress. The stalker was increasing the pressure, and Marla was beginning to unravel. Not that Nancy could blame her. Still, there had to be a way to trap the man—but how?

As soon as the girls arrived at Hollywood Gold Studios on Wednesday morning, they parked Marla's Bronco, then stayed in the parking garage to check for the stalker's van.

"It's a white minivan," Nancy said, glancing down at her list of crew members who drove similar vehicles.

"I'll know it if I see it," Marla told her as she headed down the row of parked cars.

The girls' search turned up two white minivans, both registered to guys on *Sunny-Side*'s electrical crew, and both Japanese made.

"This doesn't mean that the stalker isn't someone who works on the show," Nancy pointed out. "He could own more than one vehicle. We'll just have to keep looking," she said as they headed into the studio.

On the set of *Sunny-Side Up*, Nancy and Bess stood at the edge of the diner to watch the rehearsal. Judging by the comments that flew around, it was clear that the actors had a good working relationship.

At one point Marla and Chelsea were waiting for Tony to enter the diner, but he missed his cue. The stage manager was about to have him paged when Tony burst onto the set—through the window of the diner.

"Hey!" Chelsea said. "What's going on?"

The rest of the cast and crew were quicker on the uptake. They laughed as Tony swept Marla off her feet and carried her out through the window.

"Okay, people," Haley said, clapping as the laughter died down. "Nice improv, Calavicci. Now let's do the scene the way it's scripted."

"Killjoy," Tony joked, lowering Marla to her feet, then going off to take his place backstage.

Meanwhile, Izzy left the props table to rush to Marla's side. "Are you all right?"

"I'm fine," Marla said, taking a step away from him as she straightened her skirt.

Her senses on alert, Nancy watched from just a few feet away.

"Are you sure?" Izzy moved closer and peered at Marla intently. "You could've been hurt. He shouldn't handle you that way. Can I get you a soda? Or do you want an aspirin?"

"I'm fine," the actress repeated firmly. "But it makes me—uncomfortable when you make such a fuss over me, Izzy."

"Don't be that way, Marla," he pleaded. "I would never do anything to hurt you. I'm crazy about you."

"Izzy . . ." Marla hesitated. "I've told you before that I don't feel the same way."

"I'm sorry," he said, staring down at the floor. "You keep saying that, but you've never really given us a chance." He pushed his heavy glasses up his nose and looked up with a hopeful smile. "Maybe we could go out for dinner sometime, just the two of us."

"No," Marla said firmly. "It's just not going to happen."

There was stony silence. Then, with a sulky expression on his face, Izzy walked away.

Upset, Marla started to follow him, but Nancy came over and touched her arm. "You said all the right things," Nancy told her. "Just let him go."

"I still think he's creepy," Bess whispered as she watched Izzy adjust the props in the diner. "He never takes his eyes off you during rehearsal," she told Marla.

Marla frowned. "I just wish he'd leave me alone."

Just then Marla was called back to the set, and the rehearsal continued. As Nancy watched the run-through, she stole a few glances at Izzy and tried to compare his face to the shadowed face of the stalker. The wool cap would have covered his frizzy red hair. The stalker didn't wear glasses, but there was the possibility of contact lenses. It could be him, she thought, but she couldn't tell for sure.

As noon approached, the director decided to break early. "Let's all get lunch," Haley called. "Be back and ready to go in thirty minutes. Every minute counts since we have to cut our rehearsal short for the P.R. event this afternoon."

Nancy had almost forgotten about the autograph session. She wondered if the stalker would be there.

"Let's just go to the canteen," Marla said as she grabbed her script. "It's right on the studio lot."

Before they made it to the door, Sly Steele sauntered onto the half-empty set, his long hair bouncing on his shoulders as he walked.

"Marla!" he called. "I caught you! I don't have to tape my scene until later this afternoon. Let's grab lunch."

Nancy looked from Marla to Sly. He was the kind of guy who made demands instead of invitations.

"No, thanks," Marla told him. "I've got plans."

"Change them," Sly insisted, slipping an arm around her waist and pulling her close. He grinned at Nancy and Bess, adding, "She likes to play hard to get."

"It's not a game, Sly," Marla said, squirming out of his grip. "And I don't like being manhandled."

"Hey, I'm cool." He raised his hands defensively. "But you're not going to get rid of me so easily." He touched Marla's chin and lifted her face so that her eyes met his. "I'm going to find a way to win you back, sweetheart."

"Sly—" Marla sighed. "That's not—"

"Don't fight it," he said, touching her cheek.

Suddenly Marla lost her patience. "Just leave me alone," she told him. Tucking her script under her arm, she marched away.

Sly acted as if he shrugged the whole thing off.

"He sure is persistent," Bess observed.

"He's a pain in the neck," Marla said flatly.

"And incredibly arrogant," Nancy added. "He shouldn't be on the set."

"That's right," Bess said. "When will that new security policy begin?"

"I'm going to call Ken Zubin right after lunch to see what's happening," Nancy said as she held the stage door open for Marla and Bess. "As you two were talking, I kept trying to picture Sly as the stalker in that white minivan, but the truth is I didn't see enough of the stalker's face to make an identification."

"Hold on a second," Bess said, squinting into the midday sun. "Sly does have an alibi, at least as far as the rattlesnake is concerned."

"What do you mean?" Marla asked.

"He was already at the theater when we arrived," Bess answered. "And he sat in the row in front of us, remember? I know he didn't leave during the show."

"Are you sure?" Nancy pressed her friend.

"Absolutely." Bess blushed. "I never took my eyes off him. I mean, he *is* kind of cute."

"And after the movie, I noticed him several times," Nancy recalled. "He couldn't have been the one who planted the snake in the car. So unless he's working with an accomplice, Sly is probably not the stalker."

Nancy was upset. How was she going to catch the stalker when he left so few clues behind?

"How do we get to the studio tour, young man?" a frail, blue-haired woman asked Joe.

"Just follow this path to the end and ride the star-case down to the valley," Joe said, handing the woman a brochure with a map on the back.

"The star-case?" she repeated.

"It's a star-studded escalator that zigzags down the hill," Joe explained, hoping the woman and her friend would just take the brochure and move on. He had more important business to take care of—like finding out what Randi Jo was doing in the Camera Cave. She was assigned to information duty that day, just as Joe was. They were supposed to hand out maps and guide visitors through the park.

So why had Randi Jo just ducked into the side door of the photo center?

Joe worked his way down the path, handing out brochures as he approached the main door of the Camera Cave. Inside, he told the clerk he was just browsing.

Positioning himself behind a rack of photo postcards, Joe peered into the back room. Orlando and Randi Jo were standing in front of the enlarged photos, which were now mounted on cardboard.

"Take this photo of the costumes." Orlando slid the photograph into a large envelope. "This shot of the boy beside the sign should seal the deal," he said, adding it to the package.

Seal the deal! Joe's mouth dropped open. So they really *were* planning to sell the compromising photos of the park!

"If this doesn't do it, I don't know what will," Randi Jo said, tucking the envelope under her arm.

"Thanks," Orlando told her. "I could never pull this off without you."

"I'm just the messenger," she said. "But I'd better go before someone catches me in here."

Too late, Joe thought. You're already caught. But what were they planning to do with those photos? Blackmail the park? Or just ruin the reputation of HG Studios by selling the photos to the tabloids?

Chapter

Twelve

JOE WATCHED Randi Jo say goodbye to Orlando and slip out the rear door. He immediately headed for the shop's entrance.

Outside he spotted Randi Jo walking toward the park gate. She could be sneaking those photos out of the park! he thought. Determined to stop her, Joe wove a tight path through the strolling tourists. He was just a few paces behind her when he felt a hand close over his shoulder.

"Hey, brother," Frank said. "What's your hurry?"

Frank's navy coveralls with a tiny studio emblem over the breast looked a lot more official, Joe thought, than his banana outfit. "Damage control," Joe said, "and you're just in time to help me."

Quickly he explained that Randi Jo was making off with the photos. "I'd love to find out who she intends to pass that envelope to, but we can't let those photos fall into the wrong hands."

"You're right," Frank said, watching Randi Jo's blond head bob in the crowd. "We've got to stop her before she leaves the park."

"I'll distract her," Joe said. "You grab the photos and meet me in Sonia Gold's office."

"How are you going to distract her?"

"Never underestimate this smile," Joe called over his shoulder as he ran to catch up with her.

"Hey, Randi Jo!" He managed to head her off. "Just the girl I wanted to see. Got a minute?"

"Well, actually I'm kind of in a hurry," she said. "Can you wait till—"

"This'll only take a second," Joe said, pulling a brochure from the stack in his left hand and flipping it open to the page with the map. "People keep asking me about the best way to get down to the studio tour, and I was wondering . . ."

As he spoke, Joe moved over to a low brick wall, where he placed the brochures and spread out the map. Reluctantly, Randi Jo followed him, clutching the manila envelope under her arm.

"The best way to get down to the valley is the star-case," Randi Jo explained.

Just then, as Joe had hoped, the breeze picked up and scattered the stack of brochures. "Oh, man!" Joe said, chasing after the flying papers.

Randi Jo responded just as quickly, setting her large package down on the wall, then hurrying over to help Joe collect the brochures.

Kneeling on the pavement, Joe paused to sneak a glance back at the wall. He saw his brother dart up to the package. Then Frank dashed around the low wall and disappeared behind a trellis.

"If you grab those two in the hibiscus bush, I think we'll have them all," Randi Jo said to Joe.

He jumped up, grabbed the last two brochures, and returned to her side. "Thanks a lot," he said. He felt a little bad for having tricked her. He felt even worse when she turned to the wall and frowned.

"My package! Where'd it go?" She rushed over to the low wall and searched the area. "I don't understand what could have happened to it!"

"Gee . . ." Joe scratched his head. "You left it right there. What was in that package, anyway?"

"It was— There were some—" she stammered. "A friend of mine trusted me with something," she said, "and now I've botched up everything."

"Do you want to report it to the lost and found?" Joe suggested, hoping that Randi Jo would tell him more about the contents of the envelope.

She hesitated a moment, then shook her head. "No, it wouldn't help," she said sadly. "I guess I'd just better get back to work. You, too." She handed him the brochures she'd collected, then turned away.

Watching her walk down the path, Joe felt another twinge of guilt. Randi Jo was so sweet and cute; he hated pulling a fast one on her. If she was involved in the sabotage, though, he had to know about it.

As soon as she was out of sight, he turned and jogged through the park entrance, toward the building that housed Sonia Gold's office. He dashed through the lobby, punched the button for the fourth floor, then rode the elevator up. Frank was already there, along with Sam Tenaka and Sonia and Jason Gold. The four of them were studying the photos.

"It would have been disastrous if these had made it outside the park," Sonia said, holding up a photo of the damaged Space Race rocket. The photograph showed the safety bar hanging off the ride like a broken tooth.

"Looks like Orlando has been doing some extra work," Sam said, glancing down at the photographs.

"Is it possible that a park official asked Orlando to take these for insurance purposes?" Frank asked Sonia, who shook her head.

"I already checked with Ken Zubin. He explained that the adjusters from our insurance company take their own photos," she said. "I'd better get Dad on the phone to see what he wants to do about this mess." Sonia picked up the phone and punched in some numbers.

While she explained the situation to her father, the others searched the photos for clues.

"Orlando and Randi Jo must have intended to use these for another purpose," Joe added.

"I want them fired," Jason barked.

"Now wait a second," Joe objected. "Maybe there's an explanation behind—"

"Fire them both. We can't have photos like these leaked with the sale of the park pending. Twinkle might withdraw its bid."

"The park is for sale?" Joe asked, surprised.

"Is that public information?" asked Frank.

"It's *top* secret," Sonia said, glaring at her brother. "And before you say another word, I'm putting Dad on the speakerphone." She pressed a button, and Irwin Gold's voice boomed out.

"Sonia told me about the photos," he said. "What else do you have for me, boys?"

"We just learned that the park is for sale," Frank told Irwin Gold. "This may have some bearing on the sabotage attempt."

"I doubt it," Gold insisted over the speakerphone. "No one knows anything about the sale. The Twinkle soft drink company is trying to buy the theme park from HG Studios. My son is brokering the deal."

"Whoa," Sam said, whistling through his teeth. "That's big news."

"Forget you heard it," Sonia snapped at him. "Nothing is definite yet. In fact, I think the sale is a bad idea. The theme park is our only steady source of revenue. It would be foolish to sell it off."

"That's not true," Jason retorted. "The park is

just a big playground. It has nothing to do with the business Dad founded—TV and filmmaking."

Sonia rolled her eyes. "The bottom line is—"

"Enough, you two," Irwin barked. "This is no time to discuss Twinkle. I want to get to the bottom of this photo business. Frank, Joe, do you think Orlando Nunez and this young lady are the ones causing all these problems?"

"It's possible," Frank said, "but we'll need to check them out. They're not our only suspects, though. That screenwriter, Zoe Fortune, almost nailed me with a scythe. She's definitely a threat. Can you ban her from the park?"

"Ken is looking into it," Jason offered. "He says it'll take some time to—"

"Consider it done," Mr. Gold snapped. "I'll call Zubin immediately. I think our chief of security needs a kick in the pants. And what about our photographer and his messenger?"

"If you fire them now, we may never get the facts on these photos," Joe pointed out.

"What do you suggest?" Gold asked.

"Sonia could call Orlando in for an interview," Frank said. "Tell him that these photos were found in the park. See what he says."

"I could do that," Sonia agreed.

"And tell him that you want the negatives," Jason added. "We can't have this stuff floating around for Twinkle to see."

Sonia sighed. "News of these incidents is bound to leak out eventually. Jason, don't you think it would be better for Twinkle to hear about these problems from you first?"

"Better that they *never* hear about this stuff," Jason responded. "And it's *your* job to keep things quiet."

"Enough!" Irwin Gold's voice boomed. "Sonia, you speak with the photographer. Jason, keep your cool. And, boys, let me know the minute you get a break in the case."

"Will do," Frank agreed.

After the meeting broke up, Jason turned to Sam. "I've got to do a test run on the Haunted Holiday ride this afternoon. Can you give me a hand?"

"Sure," Sam offered. "According to the maintenance report, everything's ready to go."

"Meet me down there at two," Jason ordered before stalking off to his office.

"Haunted Holiday?" Joe's eyes were wide with excitement. "Mind if I tag along?"

"Not at all," Sam said.

"Remember," Frank reminded his brother, "we're undercover."

"I'll make it my break," Joe said, following his brother toward the elevator. "Besides, all work and no play makes for a dull guide."

"In the meantime, Sam, would it be okay if I went, too. I'd also like to ride down to the *Sunny-Side Up* studio to see if Nancy and Bess can join us," Frank said. "I bet they'll be up for a break."

113

"Okay by me," Sam said.

"Great!" Joe said. "See you at two."

"I thought you guys would never get here," Joe said as Sam pulled the golf cart up in front of the Haunted Holiday ride and Nancy, Bess, and Frank hopped out.

"We had to pluck these two out of an intense rehearsal," Sam said as he set the brake and climbed out.

"Tony is going to stay by Marla's side until we meet her for the publicity gig," Nancy said. "He promised to stick to her like glue, which won't be a problem for him."

"So . . ." Bess said, rubbing her hands together as she stared up at the contorted, batlike facade. "We're ready for some thrills and chills."

"Jason's in there setting up. I've been dying to get a look inside this ride," Joe said as he pushed open the door that resembled the mouth of a vampire.

The others followed him into the shadowed chamber, where rubbery fingers of goblins waved in the slight breeze overhead. The beam of a flashlight bounced around the entryway, and Joe followed the source of the light to Jason Gold. As Joe's eyes adjusted to the darkness he took in the eerie entryway, sprinkled with bats, spiders, goblins, and dusty webs. "Totally cool!"

"We could use better emergency lighting in here," Jason commented as he flashed the beam on the others, homing in on the girls. "Who's this?"

"I'm Nancy Drew," Nancy said. "We met briefly at the movie premiere last night. And this is my friend Bess Marvin."

"Nancy and Bess are going to help us give the ride a test run," Frank said.

"Well, then, let's give this baby some power and get started." Jason fished a fat key ring out of his pocket and opened the door of a huge grandfather clock swathed in cobwebs. Inside was a control panel. Everyone watched as Jason inserted a key and a few buttons on the panel lit up.

"I didn't realize you started these rides with a key," Frank said.

"It's a security measure," Sam explained. "Sonia and Jason both have master keys. And individual keys are signed out to people operating or servicing the rides. The key prevents park visitors from tampering with the system."

Leaning over the box, Jason adjusted two levers, then gestured to the cars. "That should do it. Which one of you wants to be the first victim of Haunted Holiday?" he joked.

"I'll go," Joe offered, jogging over to the loading platform. Already a coffin was creeping toward him along the track. It paused and Joe climbed into the red crushed-velvet seat and pulled the safety bar down.

"We'll be right behind you," Nancy said as she climbed into the front of the second coffin. Bess and Frank squeezed in behind her, pulled down their safety bars, and slid forward.

Joe was already soaking up the eerie ambience. Mad shrieks echoed through the area, and poltergeists danced along the ceiling. He settled in to enjoy the ride.

His coffin plunged down into the first chamber, a lofty crypt, and Joe was assaulted by the sounds of creaking stairs and diabolical laughter.

Before Joe's eyes, the ghostly apparition of a woman in a lace gown appeared. "Help me!" she cried, reaching out for him. His coffin lunged toward her, then at the last second swerved away toward a sarcophagus painted with colorful hieroglyphs.

"Sorry, lady," Joe tossed back to her. The sarcophagus lid flew open, and a tattered mummy climbed out, its muslin wrappings fluttering as it lifted its arms toward Joe.

Joe ducked away from the tattered linens as his coffin rose along the track, heading into the tunnel to the next chamber. Suddenly the entrance to the tunnel was illuminated, revealing the huge head of a vampire. The track disappeared into the vampire's mouth, which opened and closed with evil glee.

"Cool," Joe said out loud, bracing himself for the plunge into the entrance.

As Joe's coffin approached, the teeth began to close. The timing seems to be off, but that was probably part of the thrill, he thought.

Joe stared at the teeth that loomed overhead. Each fang was at least three feet long and coated with a metallic finish. These things really seem deadly, Joe thought.

He knew it was just a ride, but still he actually ducked lower in the coffin as the grisly mouth began to close around him. The next thing he saw was the vampire's fang as it fell like a guillotine, tearing through the wood of his coffin!

Chapter

Thirteen

Frank heard the noise first—the scraping, screeching sound of grinding metal and splintering wood. Peering around Nancy, he saw the jaws of the vampire close around his brother's coffin, biting into Joe's car like a ravenous monster.

"What in the—" Nancy gasped. The coffin was impaled on the vampire's teeth—and Joe was inside it!

"Those teeth must be crushing Joe!" Bess shouted.

Frank squeezed out from under his safety bar and jumped out of the slow-moving coffin. He remembered Sam saying something about an emergency switch, but where was it?

Dodging the robotic mummy that sprang toward

him, Frank remembered. The switch was behind the sarcophagus!

Frank bolted forward, groping along the wall. In seconds his fingers closed around a lever, which he jerked down. Instantly, the lights and sounds cut out, except for the emergency lights that flooded the area.

The chamber was deadly silent—except for the muffled growl from Joe's coffin. "Get me out of here!"

"Thank goodness, he's all right!" Bess exclaimed.

Frank scrambled up the track toward his brother. Having jumped out of the coffin, Nancy and Bess were already climbing the crest of the track, just a few feet below the vampire's mouth. Nancy scrambled up and tugged on the framework of the jaw. "It won't budge," she grunted.

Joe's arm popped out and waved. "Get me out!" he yelled, pushing futilely against one of the vampire's fangs.

"Stand back," Frank said. Bracing himself against the metal frame of the vampire's mouth, he aimed a few swift kicks at the giant fang, which was made of fiberglass. It took three kicks before the tooth finally splintered and cracked off.

Frank was helping his brother out of the coffin when he heard the commotion behind him.

"What's going on?" Jason shouted.

Sam was running along the track, his flashlight pointed down. "Are you okay?"

"Still in one piece, brother?" Frank asked as Joe eased his legs out and climbed onto the track.

"I'm all right." Joe's face was pale, but he'd managed to survive the shattered coffin without a scratch. "But I think my coffin is ready for the graveyard."

"You were lucky," Bess said, brushing dust from the back of Joe's shirt. "What would have happened if that coffin had had people in the back?"

"Really," Nancy agreed, her hands on her hips. "What's with this ride?"

"That's a good question," Jason said, heading back toward the phone at the ride entrance. "I'm going to page for help from the maintenance crew."

"I'm dying to know what went wrong here," Nancy admitted as the Hardys examined the debris. "But we have to get going." The autograph session began at three, and Nancy and Bess didn't have time to stick around. "We'll save seats for you guys," she said as she followed Bess down the track, stepping carefully.

Frank checked his watch. "I can't promise that we'll be there, but we'll try," he called, then turned back to the splintered coffin.

With a little help from Joe and Frank, Sam spent the next half hour checking the mechanism that operated the vampire's mouth.

"There's a crucial part missing here," Sam said. "There's a sensor that signals the vampire's mouth to open whenever a car approaches. It's the same type of mechanism that automatically opens a door for you at the grocery store."

"Except it's a little more important when that door is about to bite into you," Joe added.

"True." Sam frowned. "The sensor was installed two weeks ago, and it worked. The crew checked it half a dozen times since then. Now it's missing."

"This is the last straw!" Jason snapped. "We're opening this ride on Saturday, and on Wednesday it almost bites some guy in half. What's wrong with you engineers?"

Jason's concern is less than heartwarming, Frank thought. He glanced at his brother, who rubbed his neck gingerly.

"Don't blame the engineers," Frank said. "Someone has tampered with this ride."

Frustrated, Jason sighed. "This is one more reason to dump this park into Twinkle's lap. I'm going up to report to my father. Maybe now he'll see what a liability this place is." With that, he marched out.

Sam sighed. "It's going to take a few hours to install a new sensor. Then, we'll have to check every inch of this ride. Who knows what else has been tampered with."

While the others talked, Frank went outside to see if anyone was watching the ride. From past experience he knew that when people set traps, they often hung around to watch them snap. Frank shielded his eyes against the sun and glanced at the row of benches across from the entrance.

Bingo!

Zoe Fortune was sitting on a bench, her colorful skirts spread around her like a queen in her royal cloak. Apparently she'd gotten into the park.

She smiled as Frank approached. "Mr. Jason

121

Gold just came strutting out of there, and he didn't look happy. Is there a problem?"

"You tell me," Frank said dryly.

"Oh, I couldn't say," she answered. "But I think you should delay the opening. Someone could get hurt, you know."

"Would you really hurt innocent people over a screenplay that you say was stolen?" Frank probed.

Her dark eyes were unreadable as she stared at the haunted house. "You ask that question of Mr. Irwin Gold," she said. Then she rose, and for the first time Frank was aware of her height. He was six one, and she had a couple of inches on him.

"I know about your lawsuit against the studio," Frank said. "Why don't you leave it to the lawyers to resolve this?"

She ignored the question. "See you at the opening," she said, striding down the path, her colorful caftan blowing behind her.

Outside the Gold Arena, a line of tourists snaked along in front of the main entrance. "Looks like Marla and Tony have attracted quite a crowd," Nancy said as she and Bess moved past the fans.

Halfway down the line, several groups of people swarmed around a gunslinger, eager to have their pictures taken with him. The outlaw, decked out in black from his hat to his spurred boots, slung his arm around a heavyset woman in a flowered dress. A few feet away Zeke was setting up a shot of himself with three little boys.

Bess waited for Orlando to snap the shot before

she rushed toward the tall, rangy actor. "So—we meet again."

"Howdy, Bess," he said, grinning down at her glowing face. Staying in character, he slid his arm over her shoulder. "Now that I've lassoed you, I'm not going to let you go until you promise to come see our show. I want a date and a time."

"You drive a hard bargain, partner," she teased, but agreed to squeeze in the show the following morning. "Right now, we've got to hook up with Marla Devereaux. We're supposed to meet her backstage," she said quietly, not wanting to attract the attention of Marla's fans.

"Well, then, you'd better wait by the stage door," Zeke said, steering Bess and Nancy toward the side of the arena. "Catch you tomorrow."

"It's a date," Bess said, waving as she and Nancy moved away from the crowd. Still beaming, she turned to Nancy. "Will you come with me? To the Outlaw West show?"

"It depends on what Marla's schedule is like in the morning," Nancy said as she spotted the stage entrance ahead. "I'd like to see Zeke perform, though. The guy has presence."

Five minutes later a limousine pulled up to the side door, and the driver jumped out and rushed around to open the back door.

"Not a bad way to travel," Nancy teased Marla and Tony as they stepped out.

"I love this star treatment," Tony said, flipping up the collar of his leather jacket. He knocked on the stage door, and it opened, revealing a uniformed guard. After a quick check of their badges, the group went backstage.

Bess's eyes lit on the stage. "Hey! They're setting up the diner."

"That's the magic of Hollywood," Marla said. "Sometimes they go all out for these events. The better our P.R., the better our ratings."

Sonia Gold greeted the group backstage. "I'm glad you're on time," she said. "We've already got a hundred or so park guests waiting outside. This is a key media event for both the show and the park. Now, can we get a little makeup on Marla?" Sonia called, turning to some workers in the wings. "Tony, too."

"Just go easy on the blush," Tony told the makeup artist. "I play a biker, not a clown."

"Isn't there a dressing room?" Bess asked as Marla was escorted to a director's chair at the side of the stage.

Marla shook her head as she slung the strap of her large shoulder bag over the arm of the chair. "Not for a gig like this. We come in costume, and anything we need, other than stage makeup, we bring. That's why I brought this," she said, pointing to the script shoved into the outer pocket of her purse. "You never know when you're going to get a few extra minutes to memorize lines."

While Marla and Tony were being made up, Nancy checked out the stage, where crew members were swarming. Izzy Kapowski was unloading cups and plates from a large box, grips were carrying stools up to the stage, and audio technicians were testing microphones. Nancy knew this was a perfect time to learn more about Izzy. She meandered over to the side of the counter. "Can I give you a hand with those cups?" she offered.

"Nope. Props can only be moved by union people," he told her sulkily.

"That makes sense," Nancy said cheerfully. "How long have you been working props?"

"Twelve years," he answered proudly.

"It must be exciting to work in Hollywood."

"A lot of people get jaded about this business," he told her, "but I love it. I grew up watching old movies on television. The camera captures a different world—a safe, orderly place that no one can ruin." His eyes glazed over with longing as he spoke.

"Movies are fun," Nancy agreed. She sensed that Izzy spent much of his life getting vicarious thrills through film.

As he spoke, Izzy tossed the empty box aside, then reached into another crate to unload menus, condiment bottles, and salt and pepper shakers.

"You work such long hours here," Nancy said. "Have you ever considered leaving Hollywood?"

"Never!" he insisted. "I could never leave Marla. She's everything to me."

His emphatic answer sent a chill through Nancy. The guy was way out of touch with reality. There was no telling what he would do to "win over" Marla—or to harm her if she angered him.

While Nancy was onstage, a team of uniformed security guards arrived. Finally, some help! Nancy thought with relief. She went backstage to fill in Marla and Bess. "We're going to have to be extra careful here," she told them. "With all these people walking onto the stage, Marla will be in a vulnerable position."

"I've been dreading this," Marla admitted. "I hate to sound paranoid, but getting close to a few hundred strangers is the last thing I want to do right now."

"But we've hired extra security," Sonia Gold pointed out. "We've got half a dozen guards, trained to handle this sort of thing. It'll be fine."

"Well . . ." Marla finally sighed and said, "I guess the show must go on. . . ."

Five minutes later the doors were about to open to the public. "Places, everyone!" Sonia called. "Let's clear the stage."

Marla stashed her shoulder bag under the counter onstage, then she and Tony were ushered to their places backstage.

"This is so exciting," Bess said as she and Nancy sat down in the first row. The two seats beside them were marked off with tape, reserved for Joe and Frank. Then the doors were opened, and enthusiastic fans streamed down the aisles toward the seats in the front of the arena.

There was an awkward moment when Chelsea Woo strolled in and asked Sonia, who was standing in the aisle near Nancy and Bess, if she could participate in the event. "My character is pretty popular, too," she told the P.R. director. "How about a scene with the three of us?"

"Stardom gives some people a swelled head," Bess whispered as she and Nancy listened in.

"I wish we'd thought of that, but we've already rehearsed the scene," Sonia said tactfully. "Why don't you take a seat in the front row? We'll have the emcee introduce you."

Chelsea complied, though she didn't seem too happy about it.

Just as the theme music for *Sunny-Side Up* came over the sound system, Joe and Frank slid into the seats beside Nancy.

"You made it," Nancy whispered as the emcee announced Tony and Marla. They bounded onstage and immediately launched into a scene. Their lines were witty, but Nancy knew that the real attraction to fans was the romantic tension between Marla and Tony. When Tony pulled Marla close and gave her a long, passionate kiss, the audience let out an audible sigh.

"They're so great together," Bess said, clapping as the short scene ended.

Then the audience was invited to file onstage, where Marla and Tony sat behind the counter of the diner, ready to sign autographs.

"Let's go onstage," Nancy suggested. "We can keep watch and give Marla some moral support."

Joe and Bess positioned themselves on Marla's right, while Frank and Nancy took the other side of the stage. They stood beside the staircase, helping fans up.

"Can you sign the back of my T-shirt?" one woman asked Marla, who looked at the *Sunny-Side*

Up shirt the woman had obviously purchased at one of the theme park shops. "I want to take it home and frame it."

"She's not *that* famous," Tony teased.

"I'm flattered." Marla smiled at the fan. "But let me get my felt pen. This ballpoint won't work if I'm writing on your back." She grabbed her shoulder bag from under the counter and set it on top.

"The crowd seems pretty polite," Frank said.

"Let's hope so," Nancy added, glancing over the tide of eager faces, then back at Marla, who was unzipping her bag. Just as Marla was about to reach inside, Nancy noticed what looked like a hairy brown thread at the opening of the actress's bag. Was she imagining it? Nancy wondered. Or was the thread moving? Then another thread looped over the zipper—and then, a fat, mottled body appeared.

"What?" Marla jerked her hand away.

"A spider—" Nancy crossed to Marla.

"Watch out," Frank shouted. "It's a tarantula!"

"Ahhh!" Marla recoiled as another furry leg emerged. Suddenly an entire family of spiders was scrambling out of her shoulder bag onto the counter!

Chapter

Fourteen

PANIC ERUPTED in the arena.

The fans onstage shrieked and scattered, racing for the stairs, knocking over others standing in line. People in the back craned their necks to see what was happening. Joe grabbed Marla and Bess, pulling them backstage. Tony followed them, his face pale with shock.

Meanwhile, the big, hairy tarantulas were spreading out across the counter. Three—four—five—six of them.

"I'll get them!" One grip lunged forward with a board in his hand, but Izzy grabbed it before he could swat at the spiders.

"Don't hurt them!" Izzy shouted. "They're living things."

Dangerous living things! Nancy thought, searching the stage for something to contain the tarantulas. Her eyes lit on an empty cardboard box, and she picked it up and crept toward the tarantulas. Holding her breath, she turned the container upside down and dropped it onto the counter.

"You got them!" Frank called.

"Except that one!" She pointed to a stray spider, which was moving down to the stage floor. "Don't let him get away."

Thinking fast, Frank snatched a large bowl and chased after the spider. He managed to capture the creature when he overturned the bowl on the floor.

"Way to go!" a guy from the crew shouted, and suddenly the audience burst into a round of applause for Nancy and Frank.

A little embarrassed, Nancy felt her face heat up as she graciously took a bow. A clicking sound at the foot of the stage caught her attention, and she spotted the dark-haired park photographer. He was getting everything on film!

"Sonia—" Nancy rushed offstage and found the P.R. director talking with a guard.

"We called the studio's animal compound," Sonia said. "They're sending over a spider wrangler immediately."

A spider wrangler? The job title seemed odd, but Nancy had more important things to take care of. "The park photographer is getting this on film." She gestured to the front of the stage.

"Orlando! I'd better speak with him now." Sonia sent a guard over to fetch the man.

While Sonia talked with the photographer, Nancy went back onstage, gingerly lifted Marla's bag from the counter, and poured the contents onto the counter. She breathed a sigh of relief that no eight-legged stragglers were lingering inside. Just to be sure, however, that there were no spiders hiding under anything, she gingerly spread the contents of the bag on the counter. She noticed a scrap of paper with writing on it. Curious, Nancy picked it up and read the message, written in bold, block print:

ALONG CAME A SPIDER—
IT SAT DOWN BESIDE HER
AND FRIGHTENED MISS MARLA AWAY—
TO THE GRAVE.

Nancy shuddered involuntarily and dropped the note on the counter. Briefly she considered hiding it from Marla, but Nancy knew there was no way she could withhold it from her.

Nancy reassembled the contents of Marla's bag, then brought it backstage with her to check on Marla. She found the actress slumped in a director's chair, with Bess, Tony, and Chelsea gathered around her protectively. "It looks like the spiders are another gift from our friend," Nancy said, handing Marla the note. "I'm sure Detective Bolita will want a look at this, but the printing is pretty generic. It'd be hard to trace."

Marla's mouth dropped open as she read the message. "This is the end," she whispered. "I—I just don't think I can go on."

Joe read over Marla's shoulder. "Just like the old

nursery rhyme," he said. And just like Zoe Fortune's rhyming threats, Joe thought. Could Zoe be the person stalking Marla, too?

Nancy saw that Marla was shaking. A tear slid down the actress's cheek, leaving a trail of black mascara, and she rubbed her eyes in frustration. "Oh—look at me! I can't do this."

"Sure you can," Chelsea said. "We'll get the makeup person over here and you'll be as good as new, ready to continue the autograph session."

"It's not so simple," Marla said. "This guy is really getting to me. I can't sleep. I can't go anywhere without him coming after me. And he keeps getting closer. Maybe it'd be better if I left town for a while, took a break from the show."

"But the show wouldn't be the same without you," Bess pointed out. "People across America would be devastated."

"We have to think about Marla's safety," Tony said, massaging Marla's shoulders gently.

"Quincy would kill you," Chelsea said, "but I understand how you feel. I mean, if you have to choose between giving up the show or saving your life, I think the choice is clear."

Glancing at their defeated expressions, Nancy realized that time was running out. Marla was caving in under the pressure. If Nancy couldn't track down the stalker soon, Marla would pack up and leave Hollywood, ending a promising career.

"Let me get you something to drink. It'll make you feel better," Chelsea offered, patting Marla's shoulder. "I'll be right back."

Once she was out of earshot, Nancy turned to Marla and spoke quietly. "I'm not going to give up on getting this guy."

"How and when do you think those spiders got in your bag?" Joe asked.

"I—I don't know," Marla said, her blue eyes bright with unshed tears. "It couldn't have happened while I was onstage."

"Too many people around," Bess agreed.

"Then let's backtrack," Nancy suggested. "You had your shoulder bag in the limo, yes?" When Marla nodded, she went on. "When was the last time you left it alone?"

Marla bit her lip as she thought. "It was in my dressing room while we were rehearsing this afternoon. We were running late, so I just grabbed it and ran for the limo."

"That must have been when the tarantulas and note were planted," Nancy said. "During the rehearsal. So the stalker has to be an employee of HG Studios."

"But who would even want to do this to Marla?" asked Tony.

Nancy frowned. "It could have been Izzy. He was upset over being rejected this morning."

"It could have been Sly," Bess pointed out. "He's still allowed on the set."

Checking out the action onstage, Joe said, "It looks like they'll be ready to continue the autographing once the spider wrangler gets the spiders off the stage."

"Are you up to it?" Tony asked Marla gently.

The actress sighed and wiped the smudges off her face with the backs of her hands. "I'm willing if you are—at least as soon as I get made up again. But this is one time I'm going to have to do a major acting job to cover up the way I'm *really* feeling."

Meanwhile Frank listened as Sonia gave Orlando Nunez a lecture. She told him about the portfolio that had been brought to her office. She expressed concern over the nature of the photos. Finally she asked him to turn over the roll of film that he'd just shot.

Throughout her speech, the photographer's face remained impassive. He didn't even flinch when she suggested that his job was in jeopardy.

"The film, please," Sonia demanded, holding out her hand.

Orlando clung to the camera. "It's my film, and this is my break. These photos belong to me."

"What?" Sonia's eyes narrowed with indignation. "You know we don't approve of free-lancing —especially on park property."

Orlando shrugged. "Everyone in town does work on the side. Just because you run this park like a dictatorship doesn't mean I'm going to be your slave. If you don't like it, fire me."

"We will!" Sonia retorted.

"That's your choice." Without another word, Orlando turned and walked toward the arena exit.

"Wait! You owe us an explanation!" Sonia called after him, but he didn't even glance back. Frustrated, she exhaled deeply, then pushed her red curls away from her face. "He's going to be a problem."

"I'd say he already is," Frank said.

Onstage Nancy was talking with Rick Greentree, the spider wrangler. A solidly built man with short black hair, Rick moved with a cool, laid-back attitude. Armed with gloves and a container resembling a covered bucket, Rick lifted the overturned bowl and smiled. "This is Curly, and he's twelve years old." He nudged the large spider into the container. "He's one of three spiders we named after the Stooges."

"Well, then these guys must be Moe and Larry." Nancy pointed to the box on the counter.

Rick picked up the box and smiled. "Moe, Larry, and the Golden Girls," he said, scooping the spiders into the bucket. "You did a nice job catching them. A lot of people would have killed them. Tarantulas do bite, but they're not killers."

"How do you think these spiders got into Marla Devereaux's purse?" Nancy asked.

"You got me." Rick tamped the lid down on the bucket. "All I know is that the tarantula cage was empty this morning when we went to feed them. We turned the compound upside down searching for them."

So the tarantulas had come from the studio lot. Nancy had a lot of questions for Rick Greentree, and she knew Frank would want to check out the scene of the theft. "I'm a detective, and I'm trying to track down Marla Devereaux's stalker," she told him. "Would you mind if my friend and I rode back to the compound with you?"

"No problem," Rick said, smiling. "My Jeep's right outside."

While Joe and Bess stayed behind at the autographing, Nancy and Frank rode off with Rick Greentree. The Jeep bounced along the access road behind the rides and exhibits, then coasted downhill to the studio lot in the valley. At the gate to the animal compound, Rick pulled up and got out. He unclipped his ID card from his shirt and slid it into a slot, and the gate opened.

"So the compound *does* have its own security system," Frank said as Rick jumped back into the Jeep and drove inside.

"Not really," Rick said. "This gate will open for any employee of the studio. In fact"—he nodded at the ID card clipped to Frank's coveralls—"you could key your way in here. But the system does keep animals from getting out."

"Usually," Nancy added. "I'm still wondering how half a dozen tarantulas made it across the studio lot and into an actress's dressing room."

"The *Sunny-Side* studio isn't far from here," Rick said. "But I don't think our spiders made that trip without human help." He pulled the Jeep to a stop between two rustic bungalows.

"I agree," Nancy said, swinging her legs out. "I'd like to check out your compound to see how easy it would be for an outsider to sneak in."

"We'll start with my specialty—arachnids," Rick said, walking toward a shingled bungalow.

Inside, Nancy and Frank stood back as Rick dropped the tarantulas into a large glass tank.

Nancy watched as the hairy spiders scattered over the sandy terrain. "Why do you keep tarantulas on the studio lot?" she asked.

"They appear in films and TV shows," Rick explained. "All the animals in this compound are trained to perform by wranglers like me." He pointed to the tarantula tank, adding, "Curly here is a star. He appeared in *Killing Her Kindly*, *Web of Woe*, and *Attack of the Killer Spiders.*"

Other varieties of spiders were kept in other tanks. Rick showed the group the board of hooks where labeled keys were kept.

"That means anyone could come in and unlock a tank," Frank pointed out. "It's not very safe."

"It never was a problem before this week," Rick said. "We lost a snake Tuesday, and now this."

"A snake?" Nancy blinked. "It wasn't by any chance a rattlesnake, was it?"

Rick's eyes narrowed as surprise registered on his face. "It *was* a rattler. How'd you know?"

As Frank told him about the rattler in Marla's car, Nancy's mind whirled with this latest discovery. The stalker had gotten the snake and spiders from the studio—the person was definitely an insider.

Rick showed them two other bungalows, one filled with snakes and other reptiles, and another hopping with frogs, toads, and salamanders. Then Nancy called the *Sunny-Side* production office to request a ride back to the studio. Within minutes a production assistant pulled up to the gate of the animal compound in a cart. "Hi, Nancy," he said. "Hop in."

The assistant agreed to drop Nancy off at *Sunny-Side*'s studio, then take Frank back to the park. As the cart whirred down the path, Nancy turned to Frank and asked in a low voice, "How's the job going?"

Nodding at the driver, Frank murmured, "I'll tell you about it at dinner tonight. All I can say now is that Ken Zubin has a lot of holes in his system."

"That's for sure," Nancy agreed as the cart turned into the studio lot. The driver was taking a different route, but Nancy was beginning to get her bearings. She recognized the *Sunny-Side* studio ahead on the right. They were approaching from the back side of it. On Nancy's left was an open garage half-filled with vehicles.

Nancy's mouth dropped open in surprise. Inside the garage was a row of shiny white minivans identical to the vehicle the stalker drove!

Chapter

Fifteen

Stop the cart!" Nancy told the driver.

"What's wrong?" Frank asked, concern showing on his handsome face as he studied Nancy.

"Those minivans," Nancy whispered in Frank's ear as she pointed inside the garage. "They're exactly like the van the stalker drives." Just then the assistant pulled the cart to a stop and turned around to see what the problem was. "Is that the studio fleet?" Nancy asked him.

He nodded. "That's right. We use golf carts to get around on the lot, but if we have to take care of business outside the studio, we sign out one of those vans."

"I need to take a look at that sign-out sheet," Nancy said, hopping out of the golf cart.

"Good luck with Dimitri," the assistant told her.

"The guy who runs the van pool. He's a real bear. He'll chew you out before he lets you near one of his beloved vans."

"Wait a sec," Frank said, climbing out of the cart. "I think I know a way we can get past Dimitri without too much hassle." He straightened the lapels of his navy coveralls and smiled. "Maintenance to the rescue!"

Five minutes later Frank walked inside the garage and approached the glassed-in office. "Dimitri Papasergiou?" he asked, poking his head in through the open door.

"Who wants to know?" a burly man with black hair and a full beard growled.

He even looks like a bear, Frank thought. "Frank Hardy, maintenance rep." Frank extended his right hand, which Dimitri ignored. "I'm here to review the fleet—just a routine check. I need your sign-out sheets for the past month, and I'll be doing a spot check of the vehicles."

Dimitri's narrowed eyes locked on Frank's ID badge. "We do our own maintenance. What's the matter? You guys don't have enough work?"

"This is just a spot check," Frank said, folding his arms. "It'll just take five minutes. And you don't even have to get out of your chair. Now—how about those sign-out sheets."

Dimitri reached across his desk for a clipboard. "Here," he said, handing it to Frank. "The vans are open. But you're not going to find anything wrong. I run a tight ship."

I'll bet, Frank thought as he walked away from

the office. He ducked between two minivans for cover, then darted over to the open door of the garage, where Nancy was waiting.

"These are the records," he whispered, handing her the clipboard. "While you're going over these, I'll check out the vans."

"Great. Thanks!" Nancy grabbed the clipboard and disappeared behind the outer wall.

One by one, Frank checked the interior of the minivans for police band radios, but none was equipped with the special radios. Still, he knew that the stalker could own a portable that plugged into the cigarette lighter.

Meanwhile, Nancy's heart raced at the discoveries in the van pool records. Izzy Kapowski frequently used the studio vans, and sometimes he kept them out overnight.

And one of the vans had been signed out for more than a month to Chelsea Woo. "What is an actress doing with a studio van?" Nancy wondered aloud. Why did Dimitri let her take it for such a long period? Why didn't Ken Zubin, chief of studio security, make the connection when he heard that Marla was being stalked by a man driving a van like the ones in the fleet the studio owned?

These were questions worth pursuing.

Three hours later the sky was streaked with red, orange, and pink clouds as the sun set over the Sunset Strip. Seated on the terrace of West Hollywood's St. James Club, Nancy was finishing her last bite of lobster ravioli.

Across the table, Bess dreamily swirled angel hair pasta on a fork. Having received a personal invitation to attend Zeke's performance at the Outlaw West show, she was in heaven.

Frank, Joe, and Marla had already finished eating. While filling the girls in on the Hardys' case, Joe described the photos they had intercepted from Randi Jo. Then he told Marla about his close call in the Haunted Holiday coffin.

Marla listened, fascinated. "I don't envy you guys—or you, Nancy," she said. "Your jobs are so dangerous."

"We try to be careful," Nancy said. "And sometimes we have to use a trick or two," she added, telling the others about how Frank had used his badge and uniform to pull a fake maintenance check of the studio van pool. "All things considered, there's a good chance the stalker has been using a studio van. Izzy Kapowski checks them out all the time."

"I've never even *seen* the studio van pool," Marla said incredulously. "With my job, I spend my life inside the studio. And our parking garage is totally separate. It sounds like you guys have combed the entire lot."

"So Izzy uses the studio van," Bess said, lifting a forkful of pasta. "I always thought he was suspicious."

"When I asked Quincy about it, he defended Izzy. It *is* Izzy's job to drive around town and acquire props, and for that he's supposed to use a studio vehicle," Nancy said.

"Not so for Chelsea Woo," Frank said.

"Chelsea?" Marla shook her head in disbelief. "I thought we were looking for a man."

"We are," Nancy agreed. "But Chelsea might be working with an accomplice. Especially since she's had a van checked out for the last month."

"When I asked Dimitri about it, he said he'd gotten the word from Jason Gold to let Chelsea take the van," Frank explained. "And when a member of the Gold family gives an order, people obey."

"*Very* interesting," Joe said.

"It gets better," Frank added. "When I asked Jason about the van, he shrugged it off. He said it was on loan to Chelsea's mother, whose car was in the shop. He acted like it was no big deal."

"When you're a studio hotshot, you're used to getting perks like that," Bess pointed out.

"I remember hearing something about Chelsea's mother being in an accident," Marla said. "So what if her boyfriend bends the rules a little to do her a favor?"

"Besides," Joe added, "what's Chelsea's motive? She and Marla are friends."

"Well," Nancy said hesitantly, "I keep wondering if she's holding a grudge against Marla. When the pilot was taped, it was meant as a vehicle for Chelsea."

"But if I left the show, it wouldn't necessarily mean that Chelsea's character would become the lead," Marla pointed out. "After all, the concept of the show has changed. I think you're off track, Nancy."

"Maybe." Nancy shrugged. "But come tomorrow, I'm going to see if I can check out Chelsea's dressing room *and* Izzy's prop closet."

"You know," Frank said, "there's a possibility that our two cases are related. If someone has a vendetta against the studio, they might be trying to hurt Marla so that *Sunny-Side* will fail. That would be a blow to the studio."

"You're right," Joe agreed. "In fact, I was thinking the same thing when I saw the note the stalker left in Marla's purse. It rhymed—just like Zoe Fortune's threatening letters."

"But Zoe doesn't have access to the studio," Frank pointed out. "There's no way she could sneak into Marla's dressing room without being noticed."

Dubious, Bess asked, "Do you really have *any* suspects in common?"

"Chelsea?" Nancy suggested. "Maybe she's sabotaging the studio to get back at Jason for not going public with their relationship."

"Well," Joe said, "she does have a studio ID, which gives her access to the park, too."

"But she also spends most of her days in rehearsal with me," Marla pointed out. "Wouldn't she have to be in two places at once to get up to the park and rig those rides?"

"Good point," Frank said.

"The same goes for Izzy," Nancy said. "He spends his days on the set. But what about that park photographer?"

"Orlando Nunez," Frank said. "That guy is definitely involved in something. He didn't even seem to care when Sonia threatened to fire him."

"I've had to fend him off from time to time," Marla said. "But I've always considered him a typical paparazzo—determined and obnoxious."

"Remember, we still don't know what his motive might be," Joe said. "Or Randi Jo's."

"Still trying to protect her, eh, little brother?" Frank probed.

Joe's face grew flushed. "Hey, can I help it if I like the girl?"

"There's someone else who seems to be turning up everywhere," Nancy said. "Sonia Gold."

"Well, she *is* the studio P.R. director," Bess pointed out. "It's her job to be on top of things. Besides, she stands to inherit half of HG Studios. Why would she sabotage the family business?"

"Wait a sec," Frank said, snapping his fingers. "She's against the sale of the park to Twinkle. And both she and Jason have master keys to all the attractions in the theme park. Maybe she's been booby-trapping rides so that Twinkle will back out of the deal."

"You may be onto something." Joe's eyes lit up. "At the meeting today Sonia suggested that Jason tell Twinkle about the accidents. Remember? She told him that she couldn't keep things from the media too much longer."

"I don't know why she'd stalk me, though," Marla said.

Nancy turned to Frank and Joe. "Our cases aren't

necessarily related. The only thing they may have in common is that they're both taking place at HG Studios."

"That's true," Frank said, nodding at a waiter who was heading their way with a dessert tray. "But let's hope we both make some progress soon. Haunted Holiday is opening Saturday. If we don't catch our troublemaker before then, there could be a disaster."

The stalker is getting closer and closer, too, Nancy thought as she sneaked a glance at Marla. What would he come up with next?

"I could barely sleep last night," Bess said. "All I could think about was Zeke." A bright smile lit her face as she and Nancy waited for the Hardys outside the Outlaw West exhibit. Since the guys didn't go on duty until noon that day, they had decided to join Nancy and Bess for the show.

"I had trouble sleeping, too," Nancy admitted, "but it was because of the stalker. I kept waiting for him to show up." There'd been no sign of him, however. Nancy wondered if he was backing off because of her investigation.

Marla had to spend the morning trying on costumes in the wardrobe department, which she assured the girls was very boring and very safe. "There'll be at least a dozen actors and costume assistants around," she had told Nancy.

"Howdy, y'all," Joe said, grinning as he and Frank jogged over to where the girls were standing. "Ready to head out west?"

"I thought you guys would never get here!" Bess said. She turned and led the group inside.

The Outlaw West exhibit opened with a horse show. Magnificent white stallions and chestnut mares pranced around in formation—until a cowboy dressed in black galloped in, his guns blazing. He snatched a pretty young belle from the saddle of her horse and rode off with her, her petticoats flying. That set the stage for a gun battle, which the emcee called "Shoot-out at the HG Corral."

"This is the part where Zeke comes on," Bess whispered excitedly.

Suddenly gunslingers formed two lines on the main street of the ghost town. On one side were the lawmen, all wearing shiny badges and white hats. Across from them stood the outlaws, a mean-looking bunch wearing black from head to toe.

"There he is." Bess pointed to the line of lawmen, and Nancy recognized Zeke's handsome face.

"You're the outlaws who kidnapped Miss Nell," Zeke drawled. "We're here to bring you boys to justice."

"You'll die trying," one outlaw retorted.

The two lines of men stared each other down as their hands lingered over their gun belts. It was a tense moment—until someone yelled, "Draw!"

In a flash they reached for their guns. Blasts of smoke, dust, and gunfire followed as they shot it out, falling into water troughs and staggering through fake glass storefronts.

Bess was on the edge of her seat, watching Zeke.

He had scaled the side of the schoolhouse and was firing a rifle from the shingled roof.

At last the dust cleared, and the lawmen were the only ones who remained standing. A runaway stagecoach rolled into town, and Miss Nell jumped out and waved at the cheering crowd.

"And so the West was won!" the emcee announced. Everyone smiled as the actors sprang back to life.

Nancy noticed one gunslinger who wasn't moving. He remained stretched out beside a hitching post, and the bloodstain on his shirt looked real— too real. Slowly, he raised his head, which then fell back.

He wasn't acting. The gunslinger had been hit— with a real bullet!

Chapter

Sixteen

C ALL AN AMBULANCE," Nancy said, pressing her hand on Frank's knee. "That man is bleeding." Then she sprang out of her seat and raced down the aisle.

One of the outlaws had just noticed the injured man as Nancy leapt over the rail at the foot of the stands and ran across the dusty lane of the ghost town. She fell to her knees beside the injured man, who was stirring restlessly.

"My shoulder—" he groaned.

"We have to stop the bleeding," Nancy said. "I need a clean cloth."

"Cathy! Over here!" The man in black waved at the actress who played Miss Nell. She rushed to their side and quickly slipped off a petticoat.

Nancy balled the white fabric and pressed it to

the man's shoulder. From his pale face, she guessed that he was going into shock, but she knew it was a good sign that he hadn't lost consciousness.

The outlaw covered the man with his jacket, then squeezed his hand. "Hang in there, Ben."

"Some show, huh?" Ben muttered painfully as a siren wailed in the distance.

Frank appeared at Nancy's side and leaned over the injured man. "Don't move. The paramedics are on their way."

"Don't worry," Ben said. "I'm not going anywhere."

Five minutes later Ben was loaded into the back of an ambulance, which sped off to the hospital. Nancy stood back and brushed the dust from her jeans, then looked around her in surprise. She'd been so focused on helping the injured man that she hadn't noticed the flashing lights of photographers' cameras, the frantic security guards, the distraught gunslingers, the police detectives, or the empty bleachers. The guides must have ushered the audience out at the first sign of trouble.

Joe and Bess were talking with Zeke, who seemed just as broken up as everyone else. "I can't believe Ben got shot," Zeke told Bess. "Nothing like this has ever happened before."

Nancy found Frank sitting on the edge of the boardwalk, watching a detective from the forensic squad remove two slugs from a splintered lamppost. "They've already found five slugs from a thirty-eight-caliber revolver," Frank told her.

"Five slugs?" Nancy blinked in surprise. "You

mean, the bullet that hit Ben wasn't the only live round?"

"Nope," Frank said. "It's a miracle those other bullets didn't take someone else out. Think of it, with all the actors, the ushers—and the audience."

Nancy swallowed hard at the sickening realization that the situation could have been so much worse. "I guess this'll put your case in the public eye," she said.

Frank shrugged. "Mr. Gold realizes that. I just got word that he wants us to meet in his office as soon as this situation is cleared up. At the moment, though, Sonia has her hands full."

The P.R. director faced the crowd of reporters, her hands in the air as if to stave off their questions. Nancy wondered how the park would present this "accident" to the public. "Any idea how this happened?" Nancy asked Frank.

"That's what the police are trying to find out now," Frank said. "They're checking all the other guns and questioning the park's weapons expert, the guy in the baseball hat," he said, nodding at the group of men who had spread out the gunslingers' weapons on the boardwalk.

"We should go see what we can find out," Nancy suggested, and together she and Frank headed to the fringe of the group.

The police were in the middle of questioning the weapons expert, a short, stocky man. From the way his hands trembled, Nancy could see that he was upset.

"I loaded the weapons myself last night," he said,

pulling his baseball cap off to scratch his bristly brown hair. "Just like I always do. They were locked in our props closet, which I opened up this morning before the show. Other than that, I didn't let these guns out of my sight."

"Is there any way you could have loaded bullets in one revolver instead of blanks?" the detective suggested. "Accidentally, of course."

"No way!" the man insisted. "We don't use live ammo around here. I don't even know where those bullets came from."

"Was there any sign of tampering when you unlocked the prop closet this morning?" Nancy asked.

The men gave her a look of surprise. "I'm a private detective working here at the studio," she said quickly.

"I didn't notice anything when I unlocked the closet," the man answered.

"But someone *could* have broken in without leaving obvious signs. Can we check out the prop closet?"

The weapons expert led them behind the fake western-front buildings to a bungalow used as dressing rooms for the players, and the property closet, a small, windowless shack.

One detective checked the locks on the door, then shrugged. "No sign of a break-in."

Nancy and Frank checked over the locks and the doorjamb. Everything looked clean.

"Who else has a key to this?" Nancy asked.

"There's a file copy in our security office," the man said, "but it's never been used."

"Back to good old Ken Zubin," Nancy said under her breath.

Frank nodded. "Either that guy is incompetent, or *he's* the one sabotaging the park!"

Joe turned his eyes away from Sonia Gold when he noticed Randi Jo standing with a group of ushers, biting her nails. From her uniform, he realized she'd been working as an usher at the Outlaw West show. "Are you okay?" he asked her.

"Oh, Joe! It's all so awful. That actor was shot, and it's all going to be on TV and in the papers!"

"Well, you can thank guys like Orlando for that," Joe said, frowning at the photographer. "It's weird that he appears at the scene of every mishap."

"You can't blame him," Randi Jo said defensively. "News of an accident like this is bound to get around the park immediately. Besides, it looks like Orlando is going to be fired, and it's my fault."

"Oh, yeah?"

She nodded. "That package I misplaced yesterday? It was filled with Orlando's work. I was taking it to my uncle, who's a photo editor for a magazine."

"So you and Orlando were going to sell photos of the mishaps here at the park?"

"No!" Her eyes went wide with horror. "They were just samples! Orlando wanted to prove that he could photograph things besides happy tourists. I was trying to help him get a little free-lance work. Instead, the package got into Sonia Gold's hands, and she's going to fire him."

Joe didn't know what to say. The problem was, he believed Randi Jo, and that meant *he* was the one who'd botched things up.

She sighed. "Did you ever try to help someone, then end up making things worse?"

Glancing down into her green eyes, Joe thought of how that described the situation perfectly. The question was, how could he undo the damage?

Frank felt the tension as he and Joe sat down at the conference table in Irwin Gold's office.

Sonia and Jason Gold sat on one side of the table. Frank and Joe sat opposite them, beside Ken Zubin, head of security at HG Studios.

"All right," Mr. Gold barked. "Who's going to tell me what's going on?"

"My people are working with the police to investigate the shooting," Zubin said quickly. "We'll have a full report—"

"You should already have it," Irwin Gold said, glaring at the man. "I'm getting the feeling that you're not on top of things, Ken."

"It's not surprising, with a security system that's about twenty years behind the times," Frank pointed out. "In every part of our investigation, we've come across outdated and lax procedures."

Joe nodded. "It seems that a studio ID card can get an employee into any area of the park—or even the studio. There's no reason why employees can't be restricted to the areas they work in."

"That also applies to the studio," Frank said, turning to Zubin. "You promised to close the set of *Sunny-Side Up,* but so far there's been no sign of new security measures."

"We're working on it," Zubin said. "These things take time."

"What about the extra key to the Outlaw West prop closet?" Frank asked. "It's supposed to be on file in your office. Do you know if anyone used it last night?"

Zubin's face turned red. "The problem is, it seems to be missing."

"Missing!" Irwin shouted.

"And there's also the animal compound," Frank added, explaining about the stolen rattlesnake and tarantulas. "There's no excuse for that."

Irwin Gold pursed his lips, taking it all in. "Ken, it sounds like your incompetence has left our studio vulnerable to this troublemaker."

"We're talking about a huge operation, Irwin," Zubin said, holding up his beefy hands. "I can't control everything."

"But you might have stopped these mishaps with an efficient security system," Irwin said.

"Unless you *wanted* things to go wrong," Joe pressed.

Zubin flinched. "Are you implying that *I* was the saboteur?" When Joe didn't answer, he added, "I wouldn't waste my time pulling silly pranks—"

"One of those 'pranks' almost got a man killed this morning," Frank pointed out.

After a moment of silence Zubin closed his folder and stood up. "I'm not the nut you're looking for, but I can see that this is not working out. You'll have my resignation by the end of the day." He stormed out of the room. Frank wondered if the chief of security had been hiding something all along. From the start he'd been uncooperative.

"That man was awfully quick to give up his job," Frank observed. He asked the Golds if Zubin might have a grudge against HG Studios.

Irwin Gold shook his head. "I think this is a case of an employee who got lazy," he said, and for the moment Frank let the subject drop. "In the meantime," Gold continued, "what are we going to tell the media about his accident?"

"We can start by announcing that we've terminated Orlando Nunez," Sonia suggested.

"But that will make it look as if Orlando is the one who's been sabotaging the park, and that's probably not true," Joe objected.

"Still, we have to fire him, and we might as well use it to divert the media for the moment," Sonia said. "Not that we can *prove* he was doing anything illegal. But who knows what he was planning to do with those photos? Nunez is uncooperative, and he's used his job at the park as a means of helping his free-lance career. I've already sent someone to give him the ax."

Although Joe didn't trust the photographer, he didn't want to see the guy fired, especially if he wasn't sabotaging the park. But the matter was clearly out of his hands.

"You know, these incidents are an omen," Jason said. "A sign for us to close the deal with Twinkle before it's too late. Let's keep everything quiet until we get the park out of our hands. It's a liability."

"I'm still not sure I want to sell the park," Irwin Gold said.

"I think we should be honest with the media," Sonia said to her brother. "They've already run a story about the tarantulas. People are going to link these things together."

"And now that hundreds of people witnessed the shooting, the media are going to be watching the park very closely," Joe pointed out.

"That puts added pressure on you boys." Irwin Gold gave Frank and Joe a stern look. "You've got to root out the person responsible for this before Saturday's opening."

Since it was already Thursday morning, that gave them less than forty-eight hours. It's time for drastic measures, Frank thought, although he wasn't quite sure how to proceed.

"We're counting on you to catch this man," Irwin charged the Hardys. "No one in his right mind is going to pay hard-earned dollars to visit a park with a lunatic on the loose!"

"I feel so bad for that poor gunslinger," Bess said, "but I'm glad Zeke didn't get hurt."

Huddled on the sofa in Marla's dressing room, Nancy and Bess were filling the actress in on the morning's events. "We're all fortunate to have escaped unharmed," Nancy said.

"It sounds awful," Marla said. "Is the guy who got shot going to be okay?"

"I think so," Nancy said, "but I haven't heard anything yet."

"Let's turn on the TV," Bess suggested. "They might interrupt the programming to run a news flash."

Since Marla was on lunch break, the girls called in an order for burgers from the Gold canteen and settled in to watch television. Bess flipped through the channels until she came to the opening scene of a movie called *Killing Her Kindly.* "I always wanted to see this," Bess said excitedly. "It's a classic thriller!"

Marla stood up and stretched. "I have to get back to rehearsal. Tell me how the movie ends."

"And I've got work to do," Nancy said. She wanted to check out Chelsea's dressing room and the prop room that was run by Izzy, although she still hadn't thought of a way in to either place.

While Bess stayed behind to watch the end of the movie, Marla and Nancy went into the studio.

"Okay, people," the director called, "let's start with act two, scene two."

A glance at Marla's script told Nancy that Marla and Chelsea were both in the scene, which ran for four pages. Chelsea would be working for at least fifteen minutes. Quickly, Nancy retraced her steps. Chelsea's dressing room was two doors away from Marla's. Nancy stopped outside the door and, after checking both ways, tried the knob. The door was unlocked! Within seconds she was inside.

Unfortunately, her quick search turned up nothing of value. Besides a satchel of clothes and makeup, a photo of Jason Gold, and a poster from a Broadway show, Chelsea kept few personal belongings in her dressing room. Discouraged, Nancy crept out and poked her head into Marla's dressing room where Bess's gaze was riveted to the TV set. "Any news updates yet?" Nancy asked.

"No, but you've got to watch this!" Bess exclaimed. "The plot is very similar to everything that's happened to Marla."

"Like what?" Nancy sat down beside Bess.

"First the stalker appeared at the girl's house late at night," Bess explained. "Then he planted a snake in her house."

"Really?" That grabbed Nancy's interest.

"But it doesn't stop there." Bess's voice was rising with excitement. "After that, the heroine found black widow spiders in her purse."

"It *is* similar to Marla's case," Nancy agreed.

"We have to see what happens next," Bess said. "Marla's stalker may have copied everything that's in this movie!"

Chapter

Seventeen

"COPYCAT CRIMES aren't uncommon," Nancy said. Intrigued, she settled in to watch the rest of the movie. The main character, a pretty blond girl, had just fainted at a party.

"He slipped her a mickey," Bess said. "Drugs in her drink."

"Hmmm. That's something Marla's stalker hasn't tried—yet," Nancy said thoughtfully.

After a commercial the climax unfolded. The stalker rear-ended the woman's car. Thinking that it was an accident, the woman got out to speak with him, and the stalker forced her into his car at gunpoint.

When the credits finally flashed on the screen, Bess hit the mute button and stretched. "Lucky for her there was a cute police detective on the case. I love the ending, when he saves her from getting tossed out of that skyscraper."

Nancy's mind was spinning, caught up in the similarities between the movie and what had happened to Marla. "You may have hit on something, Bess," she said. "Izzy told me he's a movie buff. I wonder if he's using Marla to stage his own version of *Killing Her Kindly*."

Nancy decided to check in with Detective Bolita to see what he thought. Using the phone in Marla's dressing room, she called the precinct and was connected to the celebrity squad.

"The theory has merit," Bolita told her. "Stalkers are often obsessed with details and patterns of past crimes. And some stalkers have trouble differentiating between an actress and the part she plays on screen. That's one of the reasons actors become victims of stalkers."

"So if he follows the pattern in the film, we should watch out for some kind of poison in Marla's food," Nancy said. "Then some kind of minor car accident."

"Right," the detective said. "If someone hits her car, she should stay in it and drive to the nearest police station—or a well-lit place with people around."

"Got it," Nancy said.

As she hung up, Bess picked up the remote control and turned up the volume. "It's a news flash about the shooting at the park," Bess said as the camera panned over the blossoms that spelled out the name HG Studios at the theme park entrance.

Then Sonia Gold was shown, her face pale in the camera lights. "We will be tightening security due to a rash of small crimes," she said.

The report cut to an anchorwoman, who added, "Those crimes include the shooting of actor Ben Newton during the Outlaw West show and the attack on actress Marla Devereaux by six tarantulas."

Cutting back to Sonia, the report ended with her confirmation that the park's chief photographer, Orlando Nunez, had indeed been fired.

"They made it look as if he was the culprit," Nancy said, shaking her head. "I wonder what Joe and Frank will have to say about that."

At that moment Frank and Joe Hardy were inside the Camera Cave, watching Orlando pack.

"I really like your work," Frank said as Orlando carefully placed mounted photos into a large leather case. The photographer had just shown them his portfolio. The photos he had taken included candid shots of Hollywood stars and some action shots taken at the park.

"Thanks," said Orlando. "I've been wanting to branch out. Getting fired might be the kick in the pants I needed."

"I feel really bad about you losing your job," Joe said.

Orlando shrugged. "It's not your fault."

Time to come clean, Joe thought. He swallowed hard, then explained that he was responsible for the photos being brought to Sonia Gold's office. "I'm partly to blame, but I'd be willing to go to her and put in a good word for you."

"Don't bother," Orlando said. "I'm sick of photographing tourists. It's time I made a fresh start." He reached out, shook the guys' hands, and actually cracked a smile. *"Hasta la vista.* And be good to my friend Randi Jo." He nodded at Joe. "I think she likes you."

Joe beamed. Score one more for the Hardy charm.

In the *Sunny-Side* studios, Nancy and Bess had used the time during a short break to fill Marla in. They told her about the stalker in the movie and relayed Detective Bolita's advice. "It may be a long shot, but we can't take a chance," Nancy said.

"Remember to watch what you eat and drink," Bess advised.

"I—I will," Marla said. Her face blanched as she whispered, "I can't bear to think that someone would actually poison me. *Who is it?"* A hollow look shadowed her eyes as she glanced at the crew members scattered around on the set.

"Listen up, people," Haley announced at that moment, "the actor we hired to play the role of Mitch Dakota is in bed with the flu, and the casting agents are madly scrambling to get a replacement in time. The search is on—so tell your actor friends to call Olive in casting. She wants to start seeing people this afternoon."

"What kind of guy are you looking for?" asked Tony.

"Tall, gorgeous, and talented," answered Haley. "Now, let's get started."

"This could be a big break," Marla said as she grabbed her script and moved toward the set. "I just wish I knew someone to fit the role."

"I do," Bess volunteered, hope shining in her eyes. "I know a guy who's appearing in the Outlaw West show. He'd be perfect."

"So give him a call," Tony said, nudging Bess. "Don't be shy."

"I won't!" Bess exclaimed. "Just point me toward the nearest phone!"

While Bess went off making her call and Marla continued rehearsing, Nancy picked her way over twisted ropes of cables to the edge of the set. Quincy had given her directions to Izzy's property closet. With the rehearsal in progress, Izzy would stick to the set. It was a good time to check out his work area.

Nancy ducked behind the rear wall of the diner and stepped into shadowed, quiet darkness. She walked along the concrete fire wall, then pushed her way through the steel door.

She came to a wide staircase that led up to a loft used to store old sets. Glancing up, she could see an assortment of disassembled rooms through the cyclone fencing that enclosed the loft. There was a glazed shop window, a fake brick fireplace, and two thirds of a wrecked ship.

The prop closet was a room under the loft. Ignoring the sign on the door that said Sunny-Side

Props—Do Not Enter, Nancy unlocked the door with the key Quincy had given her.

It was dark inside, except for an eerie pool of light against the far wall. A lamp had been left on, casting a white glare over a poster. Nancy stepped to take a look at it.

She shuddered as she saw what it was. The lamp illuminated a photo of Marla that had been blown up to larger-than-life size. This was definitely creepy, she thought.

She flicked on the overhead light and looked around. The walls were lined with shelves from floor to ceiling. Boxes and bags contained everything for a diner—and more. There were dozens of catsup bottles, salt and pepper shakers, napkin dispensers, menus, and tablecloths.

Nancy walked past the shelves to the poster of Marla. A small table under the photo held a dog-eared script with Marla's name on it and a crumpled napkin that had lipstick smeared on one corner. That was unsettling enough, but the sight of a barrette with a strand of black hair clipped inside made Nancy's stomach twist.

Izzy was obsessed with Marla, and this corner of the prop room was his shrine to her.

Chapter

Eighteen

NANCY MADE QUICK WORK of the rest of her search. She didn't want to take a chance on Izzy's walking in on her.

She noticed that a sitting area had been set up in one corner of the room. There was a threadbare easy chair, a television, and a VCR. An old milk crate contained a stack of videotapes, and Nancy noted that they were all classic films. Looking through them, her gaze locked on one title—*Killing Her Kindly*.

"I'd better get out of here," she whispered. She locked the props closet behind her, then went straight to Quincy Albert's office.

The producer's eyes widened as Nancy told him what she'd discovered. "It sounds like Izzy's lost his mind," Quincy said. "I wish I could fire him and get him off the set, but my hands are tied. I can't fire the guy because he's collected a few mementos from a woman. There's always the possibility of transferring him to another HG Studios show, but those things take time—something we seem to be running out of."

"I think the police should know about this," Nancy said firmly, and Quincy agreed. He put a call through to Detective Bolita, who was alarmed by the news.

"I'll be there within the hour," he said. "I need to question Izzy Kapowski in person, and we'll conduct an official search of the prop room. I want this guy to know we're on his tail and that we're not backing off. Who knows? Maybe he'll crack under the pressure and confess."

"We've finished the spot check," Sam Tenaka told the three green-and-orange aliens at the exit of Space Race. Frank nodded, feeling a little silly talking to three creatures with rubbery orange faces and glittering green antennae.

One of the aliens nodded and motioned them toward a hidden door. "Right this way."

Inside, they found a fourth alien. She had removed the headpiece of her costume. Her green eyes and shiny black hair were a strange contrast to her rubberized alien body, Frank thought. She was watching over the control panel of the ride, along with four black-and-white monitors that showed various chambers inside Space Race.

"Hey, Sam," she said. "Who's the new trainee?"

"Frank Hardy, meet Wendy Chong," Sam said. Frank smiled. "Nice outfit."

"It's more comfortable than it looks," she said brightly. "Any problems?" she asked Sam, who was jotting notes on the maintenance record.

"Not a thing," Sam said. "Let me just fill out the log here."

Frank noticed that Wendy barely looked away from the control panel. A large key on a key ring had been inserted into a lock on the corner of the panel. "So this is the command center of the ride?" Frank asked.

"It's the brain," Wendy said, nodding. "It has to be supervised whenever the ride is operating."

Frank pointed to the key ring. "Do all the guides have keys?"

"No way! There's just one key, and it's kept in the security office when the ride isn't operating."

Frank nodded thoughtfully. At least this was one area of security that was fairly tight. But as he watched Wendy work the controls, he remembered seeing someone else flip switches on a panel— Jason Gold. Jason and Sonia had master keys to everything in the park.

Frank was still mulling over the key situation when he and Sam crossed paths with Joe outside the exhibit. While Sam went back to the maintenance center, Frank stayed behind to talk to Joe.

"Don't push, folks," Joe told the people in line for Space Race. "We'll get you all inside, and we appreciate your patience."

"I just had a flash of brilliance," Frank told his

brother quietly. "The person who's been messing with the rides is someone who knows how they work *and* has access to the park. Right?"

"Right," Joe said, smiling at a toddler.

"That cancels out Zoe Fortune," Frank said. "But what about Sonia and Jason Gold?"

"Shhh!" Joe said, peering over his shoulder. "Don't even talk like that around here. Besides, you don't have a motive for either of them."

"Not true," Frank said, pulling his brother a few steps away from the line. "Sonia wanted to go public with the accidents. Maybe she caused them so that the deal with Twinkle would fall through."

"And Jason?"

"Maybe he's causing the problems for the opposite reason, to pressure his father to sell. He keeps saying that the park is a liability. I get the feeling he'd do anything to make the sale to Twinkle go through."

Joe looked thoughtful. "You may have something there. But, boy, it's going to be tough to investigate. If they catch on, we'll be fired before we get a chance to solve the case!"

That afternoon at the *Sunny-Side* studios, the real drama was going on behind the scenes.

Nancy tagged along with Detective Bolita and Quincy Albert as they conducted an official search of the property closet.

"I'm from L.A.P.D., and I'd like to ask you a few questions," said Bolita.

Peering up at the man through his thick black-framed glasses, Izzy seemed to shrink with fear. "I—I don't know what—"

"We can use Quincy Albert's office," the detective said, gesturing toward the door.

Izzy raked a nervous hand back through his frizzy red hair, then nodded and followed Bolita out.

After they left Nancy huddled with Marla, Bess, and Tony. "You'll never believe what I found in Izzy's dressing room," she whispered, then told them about the shrine and the video.

"How awful!" Marla shuddered.

"At least now you have proof that he's the stalker," Bess pointed out.

Nancy shook her head. "It only proves he's obsessed with Marla. Unless Izzy confesses, there still isn't enough evidence to arrest him."

"I'm so worried about you," Tony said, putting an arm around Marla and hugging her close. "I don't want to let you out of my sight. How about dinner at my place in Malibu?" He gestured to include Nancy and Bess. "All of you."

"That would be wonderful," said Marla, leaning her head against his muscular chest.

"Can we bring our friends Frank and Joe?" Bess asked.

"Sure, we'll make it a party," Tony said. "And bring your swimsuits. We've got a heated pool and a hot tub."

"And why don't we bring dinner?" Nancy offered. "You won't feel like cooking after rehearsing all day." Considering the next trick in *Killing Her Kindly*—poison!—bringing dinner to Tony's would be their safest bet. Not that she suspected Tony—it was obvious how in love with Marla he was—but she couldn't take a chance on the stalker striking at Tony's place.

"Okay, people, let's get back to work," Haley said, clapping her hands.

Nancy and Bess watched as the players ran through the final scene of the day, in which the waitress and the biker sparred again.

The chemistry between Marla and Tony was electric. It reminded Nancy of the way she felt whenever her boyfriend, Ned Nickerson, was near.

After the scene the director told the players to gather in the diner for notes. Quickly the actors scrambled to the concession table for sodas and snacks, then took seats at tables in the diner. Nancy and Bess sat down on stools at one end of the counter. Marla was sitting on a stool at the other end.

"Okay," Haley said. "The opening sequence has to move much faster. Tony, pick up the pace. As soon as Chelsea walks through that door, you—"

Swiveling on her stool, Nancy glanced at the cast members, who nodded attentively—everyone except Marla. She was holding a can of Twinkle soda to her lips but was wrinkling her nose.

"Something wrong?" Nancy whispered across the counter.

"This soda—I thought it was lemon, but it smells like almonds." Marla lifted the can up to look at the label.

Almonds?

"Don't drink that!" Nancy said, springing off the stool.

Chapter

Nineteen

T HE DIRECTOR PAUSED midsentence, and suddenly all heads turned toward Nancy and Marla. "Is there a problem?" Haley snapped.

Nancy already had her hands on the soda can. "Twinkle doesn't make an almond-flavored soda." She held the can to her nose and smelled the scent of bitter almonds. "I'm afraid someone laced this soda with arsenic."

"You mean," Marla gasped, "it's poison?"

"Oh, no!" Bess exclaimed. "It's the next trick from *Killing Her Kindly*. Izzy slipped Marla a mickey."

"The only problem is, Izzy isn't here," Nancy pointed out. "He's been up in Quincy's office for the past twenty minutes."

"Are you okay?" Tony asked Marla, taking her hands. "You didn't drink any of it, did you?"

"No," Marla assured him, but her voice shook as she spoke. "Luckily, Nancy stopped me before I could take a sip."

Nancy held the soda can up to the light. It was marked Twinkle Lemon Refresher. "Did you open this yourself?" she asked Marla.

The actress thought for a moment, then shook her head. "It was open when Chelsea handed it to me."

Nancy remained cool as all eyes turned to Chelsea, whose face was red.

"I—I got it from the concession table," Chelsea stammered. "Izzy must have put the poison in before he was called upstairs."

"What next?" The director rolled her eyes. "Okay, I don't want any of you to touch a drop or crumb of the stuff from that food table."

"Don't worry." Juan, the actor who played the cook, dropped a bagel back onto a paper plate. "I think we've all lost our appetites."

"Get someone from food service in here *fast*," Haley told the assistant director. "And, please, let's finish up these notes."

While the meeting went on, Nancy took the tainted soda and went over to the concession table. All the cans and bottles were sealed, and none of the doughnuts or pastries had the scent of arsenic. It appeared that Marla's soda was the only thing affected, though all the food would have to be removed to be on the safe side.

Still, how had Izzy planted the tainted soda? There were dozens of Twinkle lemon sodas on the table; how could he have known which one would be handed to Marla?

Unless Chelsea was the one who'd poisoned the drink. Glancing across the studio, Nancy focused on the dark-haired actress, who seemed to be listening intently to the director.

Nancy hadn't thought of Chelsea much since the day she'd found her hiding in Marla's dressing room. But she was always on the set, always near Marla. Nancy had to consider the possibility that Chelsea might be working with the man who was stalking Marla. What had she said the other day when Marla had talked about leaving the show? Something about choosing between giving up the show and saving her life. Why did Chelsea think that the stalker wanted Marla to leave the show when he'd never suggested it in his phone calls?

With more questions than answers, Nancy headed out of the studio to go upstairs to Quincy Albert's office. She knew that Detective Bolita would want to have the soda analyzed by the police lab.

That night the girls picked up a large order of Thai food and drove Marla's Bronco to Tony's house, a rustic, shingled bungalow set high in the hills of Malibu. Through the trees Nancy could see the Pacific Ocean sparkling in the waning sunlight. "It's a beautiful spot," she said.

"Tony's hideaway," Marla said, pushing open the

front door. "Someday, if my career keeps going well, I'm going to get a place like this."

"Hey!" Tony greeted them. "Your friends are already waiting by the pool out back."

"And we're starving!" Joe called through the screened patio door. When he and Frank had gotten the girls' message at the hotel, they'd jumped into their rental car.

Nancy was eager to update the Hardys on her case but decided she could wait until after dinner. The group gathered at a round patio table to eat.

"What is this called again?" Bess asked as she dipped a tiny skewer of grilled chicken into a bowl of peanut sauce.

"Chicken sate," Marla answered. "And that's *mee krob,* and the mixture of noodles, sprouts, onions, chicken, and shrimp is called *pad thai.*"

"It's all delicious," Joe said.

"Thanks for having us over," Nancy told Tony. "You've got a beautiful house."

"And at last, we've got a chance to go swimming," Frank said. "We've been so busy, we haven't had time to go near the hotel pool."

"Enjoy it." Tony gestured toward the turquoise pool. "I scored this house when I got picked up on my first sitcom. After the dump I used to live in, this place is paradise."

"So," Bess said, raising an eyebrow, "have you guys heard my news?"

Joe smiled. "Something in those baby blues tells me that this is about that cowboy, Zeke."

"He got a part in this week's episode of *Sunny-*

Side!" Bess said proudly. "Marla called the office before we left, and they told her that the role of Mitch Dakota will be played by Zeke."

"That's great," Frank said. "With an agent like you, how could the guy lose?"

After dinner Tony and Marla went inside to go over their script revisions, while Nancy, Bess, Frank, and Joe used the small pool house to change. Then they settled around the Jacuzzi, eager to discuss their cases.

As she dipped her legs in the bubbling hot water, Nancy told the guys about the stalker's pattern in *Killing Her Kindly* and about Marla's drink laced with what seemed like arsenic.

"Detective Bolita should have lab results tomorrow. In the meantime, I'm confused about Izzy. He kept insisting that he was innocent."

"And he was upstairs when the tainted soda was discovered," Bess added, adjusting her bikini top, then easing into the tub.

"Who else do you suspect might have poisoned the drink?" asked Frank.

"There's Chelsea," Nancy said. "She handed Marla the soda."

"But she's a woman," Joe said. Steam rose around his head as he leaned back in the tub. "And you're looking for a man."

"She could be working with Izzy," Nancy pointed out. "Remember, she may think that she could take over the lead if Marla left the show—which might happen if we don't catch the stalker soon. At this point I'm watching both Izzy and

Chelsea." She slipped into the soothing hot tub and sighed happily. "That was our day. How'd you guys do?"

"I wish we had more to report," Joe said. "We're really under the gun to solve this case now that the public knows there's a kook loose in the park. If we don't find the saboteur by Saturday, the opening of Haunted Holiday is going to be a total flop."

"We did get to talk with the detectives who're investigating the shooting," Frank reported. "Ben is going to be all right."

"Thank goodness!" Bess said. "I'll bet Zeke is relieved."

"The police still haven't figured out who loaded the pistol with real bullets," said Joe. "However, my brother has a new theory."

"I do," Frank said. "I think that the saboteur might be Sonia or Jason Gold." When Nancy and Bess expressed their surprise, he explained his reasons. "And if it's not them, then someone with access and knowledge is carrying out these stunts behind the scenes. Joe and I figure they must be working after hours, when the park is closed."

"The park is open from ten A.M. to midnight, and the cleanup and maintenance crews work from midnight to six A.M.," Joe explained. "So we're going to stake out the place tomorrow morning from six to nine, when the skeleton crew of security guards are the only people around. Sam is going to help us."

"Sounds like you're zeroing in," Bess said.

"I want to be there," Nancy said, feeling the familiar thrill of an intense investigation. "I've gotten to know the park over the past few days."

"We could use your help," Frank said, "if you don't mind getting up at the crack of dawn."

"That's no big deal," Nancy said. "The only problem is that I can't leave Marla unprotected."

"Though there's a way to solve that, too," Bess offered. "Didn't Detective Bolita advise us to move her to a hotel?"

"It would be a lot safer," Nancy said. Especially now that the stalker seemed to be getting closer, she thought.

"You should move back into our hotel," Joe said. "It's close to the studio, and it has a decent-size security staff."

"We just need to convince Marla," said Nancy.

"At this point, I don't think we'll have to twist her arm," Bess said. "She knows the stalker's moving in for the kill. It's dangerous for her to stay at home, even with us there."

Nancy nodded and decided to call the hotel and make a reservation just as soon as she got out of the Jacuzzi. They had to move Marla to a safer place. At this point, her life might depend on it.

The sky was a dull gray on Friday morning when Nancy, Frank, and Joe met Sam Tenaka in the hotel lobby. As the group walked together to the gate of the theme park, the tension in the air made Nancy's stomach tighten. She knew the Hardys were running out of time to solve their case. They all hoped that this stakeout would be the turning point.

Since Nancy already had an ID card from *Sunny-Side Up,* the studio's lone night guard didn't ask any questions as she passed through the employee entrance behind Frank. Sam and Joe followed.

Inside, the empty park seemed eerie. The facade of the Outlaw West exhibit was now a real ghost town, Joe thought as he looked around, and the massive Flaming Inferno lurked on the horizon like a sleepy beast.

A beast we're going to conquer, Joe thought, determined to get some answers during this stakeout. It might be their last chance to catch the person causing all the harm and damage.

"Where do you want to start?" Nancy asked.

"We'd better split into teams," Frank said.

"I can take the valley level since I'm more familiar with it," Nancy suggested.

"Good idea," Joe said. "I'll go with Nancy. I took the studio tour during my orientation, so I know a little bit about that level."

"Take these," Sam said, handing them two walkie-talkies. "We'll check in every fifteen minutes or so."

"Good," Joe said, and he and Nancy walked off toward the star-case, the covered escalator that zigzagged down the hill.

Twenty minutes later they were walking down the main street of a sprawling western town. Although Nancy knew the buildings were no more than facades, she had to admit the effect was very convincing. She half expected a horse to come galloping around the bend.

"Wasn't this set used in *The Last Shootout?*" Joe asked as they headed toward the mill at the end of the town.

"Bess would know about that," Nancy said quietly. Her eyes checked every window and alley for a sign of movement, but the place was dead.

At the end of the street, they circled the Great Waterwheel Mill. On the opposite side of the mill, out of view from the main street, the channels of the brook looped up in a watery roller coaster—a log flume ride for park visitors, the only ride on the valley level.

"I love those things," Joe said, resting his elbows on the rough-hewn log fence.

"When these cases are solved, we'll all have to spend some time enjoying the park," Nancy said, glancing ahead. "I'm going over to check out the next set. I think it's supposed to be Paris."

"I'll look over by the animal compound," Joe said. "Catch you in a few."

"Au revoir," Nancy whispered.

This stinks, Frank thought. He'd been waiting and watching for more than an hour, but the only sign of life had come from the crackling voices on his walkie-talkie.

Stakeouts could be really boring. But even worse was the disappointment Frank felt over this failed attempt to flush out the saboteur. Where was he or she hiding?

"This is Sam. I'm over by Haunted Holiday. Nothing here."

"Roger," Frank spoke into the radio. "I've been watching Space Race, but it's dead as a—"

Just then a flash of orange and lime green emerged from the entrance of the Space Race. Frank recognized the alien costume.

"Frank?" Nancy's voice crackled. "You okay?"

"It's just one of those aliens from the planet Zebular," Frank answered.

"Now?" came Sam's voice. "None of the guides is on duty yet."

Frank looked again, and this time he noticed that the creature was carrying something. "It's got a wrench," Frank said over the air. "It's just leaving Space Race—and I don't think it was in there tightening bolts."

"I'll be right over," Sam said.

"I'm going after him—or her," Frank announced, then clipped the radio onto his belt and jogged toward the alien. Within moments he was only a few yards from the creature. He realized, however, that he had not been quiet enough, for the alien suddenly spun toward Frank, its green antennae waving. Then it turned and bolted off.

"Wait up!" Frank shouted, chasing the creature down the path.

Still clinging to the wrench, the alien led Frank on a twisted course past food stands and information booths. Then the creature made a sharp left and darted onto the star-case.

"Looks like we're headed down to the valley," Frank barked into his radio, then scrambled onto the frozen escalator. The stairs weren't built for chases, and Frank had to watch his step.

Good thing we're not running up, he thought.

Just then, the alien paused at the bottom of the escalator and reached down into the panel. Frank was in the middle of the flight when the escalator under his feet began to move up.

I'm swimming against the current! Realizing he was getting nowhere fast, Frank jumped over the moving rail to the shiny aluminum banister that was part of a staircase for people who preferred to walk rather than take the fancy escalator. Quickly, he slid down to the first landing. Then he plunged down the stairs.

Frank had just half a flight to go when the alien reached the valley level. It headed toward the Great Waterwheel Mill.

The alien ran behind the mill and disappeared through a door, but Frank was right behind. He followed it inside and found it climbing a steel service ladder that led to the top of the highest peak on the log flume ride. Frank took a deep breath, then started climbing, his fingers gripping the metal rungs. I've got one advantage, he thought. I don't have a giant mask blocking my view. As a result, he could climb faster.

By the time the alien scrambled onto the platform, Frank was closing in. He reached for the top rung—then saw the wrench looming over him.

CLANG! It struck the rung of the ladder just as Frank moved his hand away. Before the alien could strike again, Frank scrambled onto the platform.

At last he was face-to-face with the alien. "Give it up," Frank growled, reaching forward to grab the creature by the arms. He couldn't wait to pin the alien down, rip off the mask, and finally see the face of the person who'd been wreaking havoc at the park.

The creature twisted one arm free then and swung the wrench at Frank's head.

"Look out!" Nancy cried from somewhere below.

Frank ducked in the nick of time, but the sudden movement threw him off balance. His arms flailed as he tried to catch himself, but it was useless. The next thing he knew, he was falling back—back—back . . .

Chapter
Twenty

W HOA!" FRANK SHOUTED as he toppled onto the ramp that carried the log-shaped cars into the pond.

Nancy looked up from where she was standing on the bottom of the ramp and saw him sliding toward her. Quickly, she moved to the side, and Frank whizzed by her.

Behind her, Joe wasn't so lucky. Frank knocked into him, and they both slid down the final slope and landed in the pond at the foot of the water-wheel with a loud splash. A quick glance told Nancy that they were fine, but the alien was already descending the ladder—it was getting away!

Climbing on all fours, Nancy scaled the rest of the ramp to the platform and saw that the alien was already halfway to the ground. She followed it down the ladder, then tracked it away from the mill to the star-case.

Just as the creature was within a few feet of the escalator, someone emerged from behind a bush.

It was Sam!

Sticking his leg out, Sam tripped the creature. Nancy wanted to shout out a cheer when the alien toppled forward and landed facedown on the ground.

A second later it was up and running again. The escalator was on, moving up, and the alien raced up the steps. Sam chased it until the alien hurled the wrench down at him. It was enough to send Sam leaping onto the nearby stairs.

Before Nancy or Sam could resume the chase, the alien was rising out of sight.

"We lost it," Nancy said, sighing as she walked up the stairs to meet Sam.

"I'd better radio security," Sam said. "Maybe they can stop the alien at the gates."

"I can't believe he got past us," Nancy said.

"Yeah, well, at least you're dry," came a voice from behind her. Joe Hardy was dripping wet, his blond hair matted to his head. Frank was also soaked. He gathered the front of his shirt and wrung it out. "I'd rather be wet than dead. For a minute there, I wasn't so sure."

"I'm glad you're all right," Sam said, "but I'm sorry the alien got away. He had a big advantage over us, though. Not only did he have access to the wardrobe department, but he also had a key to the star-case. That's a person with some power at HG Studios. Maybe it's old Irwin himself!"

"Yeah, right," Joe said, snickering.

"There's one thing I know," Frank said. "We had pretty much discounted Zoe Fortune as the saboteur. It's definite now that she's not. And neither is Ken Zubin."

"How do you know?" Nancy asked.

"Simple. That alien was about six inches shorter than me. Ken Zubin is stocky and short—no more than five foot four. And Ms. Fortune is taller than I am. That alien was someone of average height—maybe five seven or five eight."

"Close to the height of both Sonia and Jason Gold," Joe pointed out.

"Hold on a second." Sam's eyes narrowed as he held up his hands. "Don't tell me that the boss's son and daughter are suspects now."

Joe shrugged. "They're the only people with total access to the park—besides the chief of security." He went on to explain about the infighting between Sonia and Jason.

"Just proceed with caution," Sam warned the Hardys. "If Sonia or Jason finds out you're investigating *them,* they'll have you bounced from the park like that." He snapped his fingers.

"In the meantime let's check with the guard to see if either of them was seen entering the park," Frank said.

"You might want to check the wardrobe department, too," Nancy suggested. "The alien might have inadvertently left some clues behind."

"Good idea," Frank said. "Want to come along?"

"I'd better get over to the *Sunny-Side* studio," Nancy said, checking her watch. "It's quarter to eight, and I promised to meet Marla there for her eight o'clock call."

"And I'd better get up to the park level and close down Space Race," Sam said. "I've got to go over the ride with a fine-tooth comb and undo any damage that alien did with its wrench."

Employees were trickling onto the HG Studios lot as Nancy made her way back toward the TV studio. As she walked, her mind switched back to her own case, and the seeds of a plan began to grow. She was sure that Izzy was the stalker, but how could she prove it?

If she wanted to catch him, she would have to play his game. What was the next trick in *Killing Her Kindly?*

"Kidnapped from her car," Nancy said under her breath as she tugged open the stage door to the *Sunny-Side* studios. "Let's see how well Izzy Kapowski knows his films."

Nancy went directly to Marla's dressing room, where Bess was helping the actress learn her lines. The girls' mouths dropped open when Nancy told them the details of her plan.

"We'll need a brunette wig from wardrobe," she told Marla. "And I'll need to borrow your Bronco and your clothes. You and I are the same size and we have similar features, so if we set this up right, I think he'll go for it."

"It's too dangerous," Bess objected. "You can't use yourself as bait, Nan!"

"I won't get out of the car," Nancy assured her. "And I'll lead him back to Marla's apartment—where Detective Bolita will be waiting."

"It's awfully risky." Marla bit her lip. "But it would be great to have the stalker behind bars. Are you sure you want to go through with it?"

"Positive," Nancy insisted. "We can pull this off! All we need are a few props, support from the police, and a great acting job from Marla."

"It'll be the performance of my life," Marla promised.

"Good," Nancy said firmly. "Let's do it."

An hour later Haley stopped rehearsals for a short coffee break. "Fifteen minutes, people."

"I might be a little late," Marla told the director. "I left some papers for my agent at home, and I've got to pick them up before lunch."

Nancy tried to appear nonchalant as she watched the cast and crew listen in on the conversation. Izzy's eyes were unreadable behind his thick glasses.

Haley frowned and rolled her eyes. "All right, but make it quick."

"I'll be back before you know it," Marla tossed over her shoulder as she followed Nancy out of the sound studio. Behind them, Bess reluctantly left Zeke's side to join the other girls in Marla's dressing room.

Once they closed the door, they moved quickly. Bess pinned Nancy's hair up and helped her pull on a brunette wig that was styled like Marla's hair. Meanwhile, Nancy took off her blouse and slipped on the baseball jersey and vest that Marla had been wearing. After that, she put on a baseball cap, tugged the bill over her forehead, and stood beside Marla at the mirror.

"You could be my twin," Marla said. "Boy, am I glad you're not in the union. The competition would kill me."

"Did you get Detective Bolita on the phone?" Nancy asked Bess.

"I'm on hold," Bess said. "Maybe you should wait, just to be sure—"

"There's no time," Nancy said. "Just tell him to wait outside Marla's apartment. I'll lead the stalker to him."

Bess frowned. "But what if—"

"I'll be fine," Nancy insisted.

"Good luck, Nancy," Marla said as Nancy picked up Marla's car keys and slipped out the door. "And please be careful."

Keep your cool. Don't walk too fast. Nancy tried to look casual as she walked out to the studio garage and hopped into Marla's Bronco. It was hard to ignore the pounding of her heart, though.

He was following her—she knew he was. It would be the last time he ever stalked anyone.

Nancy was only four blocks from the studio when she spotted the car trailing her. It wasn't one of the studio's white minivans, but a dark blue sedan. That makes sense, she thought as she turned a corner. Izzy wouldn't want anyone to be able to track the studio van this time.

When the blue car turned behind her, she knew he had taken the bait.

Tapping the brakes, Nancy rolled to a stop sign on a quiet street. She wasn't surprised when the blue car crept up behind her and tapped the Bronco's bumper, jolting Nancy.

Darting a look in her rearview mirror, Nancy tried to make out the driver's face, but his car was too low and beyond her line of vision. In her side view mirror, she could see the driver's door swing open. A man in a denim shirt, heavy work gloves, and a dark knit cap got out of the car and approached her.

She looked for Izzy's fuzzy red hair under the cap—but saw, instead, chin-length black hair.

"Chelsea," Nancy whispered as she recognized the young actress. She'd guessed wrong! Chelsea was the stalker.

Before Nancy could react, her world exploded with a shattering sound and a spray of glass pellets. She's breaking the window! Instinctively, Nancy closed her eyes and lifted her hands to cover her face as Chelsea hit the window again, sending more glass flying.

Nancy had no time to react. Chelsea reached in through the opening and pressed something against

191

her temple. Pellets of glass were still jangling to the pavement when Nancy lowered her fingers to peer in the side view mirror. The object pressed against her temple was a small automatic, shiny and deadly.

Chelsea's voice was icy. "Put your foot to the pedal and you die."

Chapter

Twenty-One

Fear sent a wave of nausea through Nancy as Chelsea cocked the gun. She had to get out of this—but how?

None of her karate moves would work while she was strapped into the car. She briefly considered popping the door open to knock Chelsea down, but in the time it would take to pull the door handle, Chelsea could easily pull the trigger.

For the moment Nancy was trapped.

"Don't try anything stupid, Marla," Chelsea said, reaching over to turn off the ignition and yank out the keys.

"I'm not Marla," Nancy said, looking Chelsea in the eye. "So you can put down the gun."

The actress momentarily lost her composure. "Nancy! What are you— You look just like Marla."

"And you look just like the person who's been stalking Marla," Nancy answered, taking in Chelsea's mannish clothes, from her black combat boots to her wool cap. A consummate actress, Chelsea had dressed like a man and fooled everyone. "The only thing I don't understand is the voice on the phone," Nancy added. "I was sure it was a man's voice on Marla's answering machine. So were the police."

"I know other actors, and we've all been screwed by at least one agent. The guys who left those messages thought they were helping me get revenge on an agent. But I don't have time to explain to you. Out of the car," Chelsea snapped, unlocking the door and tugging it open.

Nancy did as Chelsea ordered, sending round pellets of glass falling from her lap and skittering along the pavement as she stepped out.

"Now walk to the back of my car," Chelsea said, keeping the gun leveled at Nancy. As Nancy walked to the rear of the car she wished for a passing car or truck, but the intersection was deserted. Chelsea popped open the trunk, then waved the pistol at Nancy. "Get in," she ordered. When Nancy hesitated, she added, "Or do I have to push you?"

Never taking her eyes off Chelsea, Nancy climbed in and watched as the actress slammed the trunk lid shut.

Then there was only darkness and the rumble of the engine as the car took off down the road.

* * *

In the circular drive in front of the tower housing HG Studios headquarters, Frank and Joe Hardy jumped off the back of a golf cart.

"Thanks for letting us hitch a ride," Frank called to the driver. The man nodded and took off.

"Well," Joe said as he glanced up at the towering glass building, "here goes. We're playing for the jackpot. Let's hope that one of the Golds doesn't call our bluff."

"The saboteur has to be either Jason or Sonia," Frank said firmly. "The security guard said they both arrived on the lot before six-thirty this morning. They're the only ones with keys to everything, and there was no sign of a break-in at the wardrobe department."

"I know all that," Joe said defensively. "But we don't know *which* Gold is the culprit."

"It's bound to come out if we corner them," Frank said, walking toward the doors.

"What if they trump up some story to persuade 'Daddy' to fire us?"

"It's a chance we'll have to take," Frank said, holding the door open for his brother.

The Hardys rode the elevator to the fourth floor, where Sonia and Jason Gold each had a corner office. When Frank and Joe paused at Jason's secretary's desk, they saw that his office was dark.

"We're here to see Jason Gold," Joe told her.

"He's not in yet," she said, then glanced up from her keyboard and frowned. "How did you two get so wet?"

"It's a long story," Joe said, turning away.

At the far corner of the hall they had better luck. Sonia was in and agreed to see them immediately.

"Rather than waste your time, I'm going to get right to the point," Frank told Sonia, who sat back in her chair and listened politely. "We've narrowed down the park saboteur to two suspects—you and your brother."

"That's ludicrous!" Sonia's green eyes flashed indignantly. "Jason and I stand to inherit HG Studios. We'd never sabotage our own dreams."

"But you and your brother *have* been arguing over the sale of the park," Frank pointed out. "Maybe he's been staging these incidents to convince your father what a liability the place is. He's said that himself."

"Or maybe *you*'ve been causing the accidents so that Twinkle realizes the park has problems and backs out of the deal," Joe said.

"After five days of snooping around our park, this is the best you can do?" Sonia retorted.

"The facts are there," Frank said. "You and your brother are the only ones with total access to the park. Who else could have put those bullets in the gunfighter's pistol? Tinkered with those rides and exhibits? None of the exhibits has been broken into."

"And you were both on the lot this morning when Frank and I came close to getting killed by someone in an alien costume," Joe added.

"What are you talking about?" Sonia demanded. Frank told her what had happened, but she still wouldn't budge. If Sonia was the saboteur, she had a heart of stone. If her brother was the guilty party, she was incredibly naive.

"I've heard enough." She stood behind her desk and pointed toward the door. "You'd better leave. I have work to do, which includes talking to my father about dismissing both of you."

Frank and Joe silently filed out of the office.

"I knew it!" Joe muttered once they were in the corridor. "Mr. Gold's going to fire us before we solve the case." They were halfway down the hall when he noticed a sign for the men's room. "Hey, wait a second. I want to wash up. Ever since we took that dive down the log flume ramp, I've felt like pond scum."

The brothers ducked inside, went to the sinks, and soaped up their arms and faces.

Frank splashed water on his face and reached for a paper towel. "I say we go up to Mr. Gold's office and tell him what we've learned. He's a reasonable—" As he tossed the balled-up paper towel into the trash bin, he saw a green-and-orange face staring up at him.

"What's wrong?" asked Joe.

Frank reached into the can and pulled out the alien's head. "Our friend from Zebular was here," he said wryly.

"The costume! Jason must have ditched it in here while we were talking with Sonia."

"He's our man," Frank said, fishing the rest of the costume from the trash and tucking it under his arm. "Let's get him."

They rushed down the hall to Jason's office, but his secretary shook her head. "You just missed him."

"Where'd he go?" Frank asked, leaning across her desk.

"I—I don't know." She shrugged, sensing the urgency. "I can have him get back to you when—"

Before she finished her sentence, Frank had circled her desk and was marching into Jason's office. Joe was right behind him.

"Hey! You can't go in there," the secretary called, following them.

Frank went directly to the datebook open on Jason's desk. "He didn't have any appointments this morning," he said, scanning the calendar. "Where is he?"

"If you must know, he got a personal call from his girlfriend," the young woman explained.

"Chelsea Woo?" asked Joe. He was fiddling with one of the pulls on Jason's desk drawer.

The secretary nodded. "She was upset. I think he was going to meet her somewhere. Hey! Don't you have any respect for privacy?"

Unable to resist, Joe had slid open the top drawer for a look. "Criminals don't deserve privacy," he told her.

"I— You guys are— I'm calling security," the secretary said, ducking out the door.

"Good. Maybe they can help us track Jason down," Joe muttered.

There was nothing unusual in the top drawer, but when Frank opened the tall drawer on the bottom, he hit the jackpot. "Tools," Frank said, checking out the assortment of wrenches. "Must have come in handy when he had to adjust the mechanisms on those rides."

In the back of a drawer was a cardboard box. Frank opened the flap, and dozens of bullets gleamed in the light of the office.

"Thirty-eight-caliber bullets?" Joe asked.

"Yep," Frank said. "Looks like we've found our man."

Joe nodded. "Bull's-eye."

Chapter

Twenty-Two

FRANK AND JOE were still searching Jason's desk when Sonia Gold walked in, Jason's secretary a few paces behind her.

"I thought I told you to leave," Sonia snapped. "Do we need to call security?"

"You probably should," Joe said. "And tell them not to let your brother leave the area. *He's* the one who's been sabotaging the park."

Sonia was still skeptical, but her manner changed when they showed her the alien costume, the tools, and the bullets. "Could it be a mistake?" she asked shakily. "I mean, I know the deal with Twinkle was important to him, but I never thought he'd go this far."

"It's no mistake," said Frank. "And we've got to find him before he does any more harm." Frank turned to the secretary. "Where was he going?" he asked the woman again.

"To meet Chelsea," she said. "I don't know where."

Sonia crossed to the window and looked down on the headquarters parking lot. "There he is! He's just leaving."

Frank spotted Jason walking toward a red Porsche and a black Jaguar in the far corner. "We need to follow him."

"You can use my car," Sonia said. She raced out of the room and returned moments later with the car keys, which she tossed to Joe. "It's the red Porsche parked next to his Jaguar."

Joe caught the keys in midair. "Thanks," he called as he and Frank raced out the door.

Five minutes later they were following Jason along Laurel Canyon, a road that snaked into the Hollywood Hills.

"Jason Gold drives like a maniac," Joe said, pushing down on the gas to catch up on the short stretch of straight road.

"You're doing a good job keeping up with him," Frank told his brother.

"This car is a mean driving machine," Joe said. "Jason's Jag doesn't stand a chance."

Glancing around the sleek interior, Frank realized that Sonia had to have a cellular phone in her car. Every hotshot in L.A. did. He opened the leather console, and there it was. "Let's check in with Nancy," Frank said, punching in the number of *Sunny-Side's* studio. The receptionist put him through to Marla's dressing room, and Bess answered. "I just wanted to tell Nancy that—"

"She's not here!" Bess cried. "We think the stalker got her. It's awful," she said, then the story about Nancy's plan came tumbling out. "The police found Marla's Bronco sitting in an isolated intersection—empty! The driver's side window was smashed!"

"Izzy's got Nancy?" Frank exclaimed.

"What?" Joe said, slowing to negotiate a hairpin turn.

"No! Not Izzy," Bess said over the line. "He's here on the set. The stalker must be Chelsea!"

"Chelsea? We're on our way to see her," Frank said. "At least, that's where we think we're going." He explained what they were doing.

"Oh, you've got to get to Chelsea in time!" Bess exclaimed.

"We're trying," Frank said, glancing over at Joe. "I'll call you the minute we know something."

As soon as Frank hung up, his brother nodded at the phone. "You'd better call the police and tell them we're headed for a showdown."

"Got it," Frank said, punching in 911. "Now, if I could only figure out where we are . . ."

It feels like we've been driving forever, Nancy thought as the car hit a bump in the road. She'd had enough time to pull off the wig and work the pins out of her hair, but the trunk was cramped and uncomfortable. The stale, hot air made her head spin, but that was minor compared to the panic welling up inside her. She was being hauled off to some deserted place by a maniac with a gun!

The car jerked forward again, then rolled to a stop. Nancy wondered if they were waiting at an intersection—until she heard the car door open. A moment later the trunk lock clicked, and bright sunlight spilled in.

"Okay," Chelsea said. "Out of the car."

Blinking, Nancy gave herself a moment to take a deep breath of fresh air and let her eyes adjust to the light. Then she climbed out, Chelsea a few yards away with her pistol pointed at Nancy. She'd taken off the gloves and wool cap, and her features were rigid and set.

They were at the top of an isolated hill, the car parked in a patch of tall weeds not far from what was obviously a dropoff.

I've got to keep her talking, Nancy thought. She had no idea what Chelsea planned, or whether the police would be able to find them. Her instincts told her to stall, though.

"This way," Chelsea said, pointing toward the cliffside with the pistol for emphasis.

I can't argue with that, Nancy thought as she walked slowly toward the edge of the cliff. Her pulse raced as she glanced down the hillside. She could see the top of the letters in the Hollywood sign. Below that, the valley seemed so far away.

"The view is great from here," Nancy said.

"No jokes," Chelsea snapped. "You've spoiled my whole plan. It was going to be so dramatic. All of Tinseltown would have been talking about how Marla Devereaux met her death at the foot of the Hollywood sign. Now that you've gotten in the way, I'll have to think up another final scene for her."

"You've been very clever," Nancy said. "But I don't understand what you think you'll gain by hurting Marla."

"At first I thought I would just scare her into leaving L.A., so I could be the lead again."

So that was her motive—just as Nancy had guessed. Chelsea acted so sweet that no one realized how crushed she'd been when the show was redone to focus on Marla's character.

"But Marla refused to be frightened off," Nancy said. "She wouldn't leave, so you took things a step further."

Chelsea smiled. "How'd you like the rattler and the tarantulas?"

"The spiders really stole the show at the autographing," Nancy said. "You must have had a lot of guts to go near them."

"I did a desert documentary last year. The wranglers on the set taught me how to handle spiders and snakes, so that was no big deal. And with the shoddy security in the animal compound, it was easy to snatch them."

Suddenly Nancy realized what Chelsea had been trying to do the day she'd found her in Marla's dressing room. "You were going to put the snake in Marla's dressing room—until I came in and found you hiding there."

Chelsea shrugged. "You got in the way of a few of

my plans. If it weren't for you, Marla would be dead by now."

"And the arsenic?" Nancy prodded.

"You almost caught me on that one, too. But by then, I guess you were onto the pattern from *Killing Her Kindly.*"

Nancy nodded. "Which you chose because it was one of Izzy Kapowski's favorite movies. You were setting him up for the fall."

"Izzy's such an oddball," Chelsea scoffed. "The perfect patsy."

"But now that you came after me, Izzy will be cleared," Nancy pointed out. "And everyone is going to learn that you were the stalker."

"Not true," Chelsea snapped, the muscles in her face tensing as she wrapped both hands around the gun. "No one knows. Once I finish with you, Marla will be easy. And then I can get on with my career!"

"Bess and Marla know that you're the stalker," Nancy said. "And by now the rest of the cast must have found out. The police are probably on their way here right now."

"That's not true!" Chelsea cried. "You're bluffing."

Seeing that Chelsea was getting dangerously upset, Nancy realized she needed to take a different tack. "Look," she said, keeping her voice calm, "you can't get away. You'd be better off—"

Before Nancy could finish her sentence, Chelsea came barreling toward her.

"That's enough!" Chelsea shouted. She shoved Nancy, knocking her to the ground.

Realizing she was only a few feet from the edge of the cliff, Nancy scrambled onto all fours. Just as she was on her knees, about to stand, Chelsea aimed a kick at her head.

Nancy caught Chelsea's boot with both hands. They struggled for a moment, then Chelsea pulled her foot free, reared back, and shoved Nancy's shoulder.

In a shower of sand and pebbles, Nancy plunged straight down the cliffside.

Chapter

Twenty-Three

N ANCY FLAILED at the cliffside, trying to find a handhold. Her fingers groped for anything to hold on to, but the sandy soil crumbled at her touch.

She was sliding past a twisted sapling growing out of the side of the hill and thrust out a hand to close around the smooth bark of the small tree. She raised her other arm and clung to the tree with all her strength, her feet dangling in midair.

Just hold on! she told herself.

Above she heard the roar of a car engine and the squeal of tires as it came to a stop. A car door slammed, and a man's voice boomed in the eerie stillness.

"What's going on here? Did I just see you push someone over that cliff?" he demanded.

"Don't worry about that, sweetheart," Chelsea said with an icy coolness.

It must be Jason Gold, Nancy thought, desperately clutching the sapling. I wonder if he's been working with Chelsea?

"I'm taking care of everything," Chelsea added. "We won't have to wait much longer. Soon Marla will be off the show, you'll be working as a producer, and I'll be the star."

"What?" he snapped. "Marla is the best thing that ever happened to *Sunny-Side Up*. I told you that we can look into developing something else for you, but we can't afford to lose Marla."

So he *wasn't* helping Chelsea. He didn't even know that she was stalking Marla.

"I'm tired of waiting," Chelsea said. "You haven't delivered on any promises yet. You won't tell your father about me, and we can't go anywhere in public. You keep talking about helping me, but nothing ever happens. I decided to help myself by getting Marla out of the picture."

"What?" His voice rose. "Are you saying that *you're* the stalker?"

Nancy couldn't hear Chelsea's answer. It was drowned out by the roar of another car engine.

Please, let it be the police! she pleaded silently, her arms growing heavier.

As the Porsche skidded to a stop in a cloud of dust, Frank jumped out and searched the hilltop for Nancy. Where was she? Jason had squared off with Chelsea, but Nancy was nowhere in sight.

Joe leapt out of the car and walked over to the couple. "The game is over, Jason," he said. "We've got enough evidence to prove that you're the one who's been sabotaging the park. The police are on their way."

"What?" Chelsea spun around and stared at her boyfriend with narrowed eyes. "You've screwed things up at the studio? And the police are coming?" Her face was taut with tension. "I'm getting out of here." She turned toward her car.

Jason put a hand on her shoulder to stop her, when a voice called out, "Frank! Joe!"

"It's Nancy!" Frank followed the sound to the edge of the cliff. Nancy stared up at him, her hands gripping a twisted sapling.

"Help me," she cried, her voice a tired plea.

Frank's heart wrenched at the sight of her. Immediately, he fell to his knees, but she was too far down to grab.

"Hold on," he told her. "I need Joe's help."

A few yards away Joe was dealing with Chelsea and Jason. "You're not going anywhere," Joe told Chelsea. He strode forward.

"Oh, yeah?" She reached into her waistband and produced an automatic pistol, which she aimed right at Joe's heart. "And how're you going to stop me?" she added with a smug smile.

Frank felt his body tense as he eyed the pistol. Things were not going well at all.

"Are you crazy?" Jason said. "Put that thing down and . . ." His voice trailed off when Chelsea spun around and pointed the pistol at him.

209

"Back off, Jason." Her face twisted in a sneer. "I'm not taking your advice anymore. Ha! If it were up to you, I'd be old and gray before I got a decent role."

The moment of truth, Frank thought. In her anger, Chelsea had turned away from Joe, who was close enough to make a move.

"Jason won't be any help to you now, Chelsea," said Frank. "He's lost his power at HG Studios."

"Don't listen to him," Jason insisted.

Frank could see his brother edging up behind Chelsea. In just a few more seconds . . .

"Even if I did meddle with a few rides in the park," Jason continued, "what can they do to the son of Irwin Gold?"

Just then Joe landed a kick at Chelsea's wrist. The actress gasped as the gun went flying.

Frank heard the wail of distant sirens as he rushed over to grab Chelsea's pistol from the sand. Jason raised his hands in surrender.

"I can't fight a bullet," he said.

Joe removed the keys from the ignitions of both Chelsea's and Jason's cars.

Tears streamed down Chelsea's cheeks, and she buried her face in her hands. "It's not fair. It's not fair," she said, sobbing.

Just then Joe saw two police cars, lights flashing, appear on the crest of the hill. "The police are here," Joe said, his voice filled with relief.

"Not a moment too soon," Frank said, nodding toward the cliffside as he tucked the gun into his waistband. "We have to rescue Nancy." He had no idea how long she'd been hanging there, but from the strain on her face he knew she couldn't last much longer.

The brothers rushed to the edge of the cliff, where Joe fell to his stomach and peered down. "Hold my ankles," he ordered.

Frank grabbed on to Joe's ankles, then sat on the ground, leaning back to anchor himself firmly.

Joe pushed himself over the edge until most of his body was hanging down. The blood was rushing to his head, but he ignored it as he reached for Nancy.

Gritting her teeth, Nancy eased one hand off the sapling and reached up, straining to touch Joe's hand. His clasp was tight, giving her the courage to take her other hand off the tree and reach up again.

Now she was dangling from Joe's arms.

"Okay," Joe shouted up. "Bring us up."

Digging into the ground with his heels, Frank pulled back, sliding over the ground a few inches at a time. In the background, he heard the sounds of car doors slamming and of police officers shouting. But all his concentration was on rescuing Nancy. Slowly, Frank dragged Joe over the edge of the cliff and then Nancy.

At last the three of them were on solid ground.

"Thanks, guys," Nancy said as she stood up and brushed her red-gold hair away from her face. "You saved my life."

"Anytime," Joe said with a cocky smile.

"I was getting worried," Frank said, putting his

arms around Nancy and giving her a hug. "I hated leaving you hanging there, but we were working at gunpoint up here."

"I'm just glad you came," Nancy said, hugging Frank back. "How did you find me?"

"That's a long story," Joe said as Detective Thomas Bolita approached them.

Nancy peered behind him and saw two officers standing beside Chelsea and Jason.

"What have we here?" the detective asked.

"We've snagged the stalker," Nancy told him, and nodded in the direction of Chelsea. "It was Chelsea Woo. She confessed everything."

"And Jason Gold has been sabotaging HG Studios Theme Park," Frank added. "There's a slew of evidence in his office."

"Is that so?" Bolita seemed impressed. "That one isn't my case, but I've seen the news reports. How did you manage to track these two down?"

Frank smiled. "It's all in a day's work."

"I'm going to miss this sunny L.A. weather," Bess said, gazing up at the clear sky.

"Maybe you should think about spending more time here," Zeke said, putting his arm around Bess's waist.

Bess sighed. "I wish I could." She looked up at Zeke and gave him a dazzling smile. "Maybe you could think about coming to River Heights. I can't promise you the same kind of excitement we've had here, but . . ."

Behind her, Nancy was talking to Frank and Joe

as they walked along the path. "I'm glad that we got a nice day for the opening of Haunted Holiday," she said. She turned briefly to make sure that Tony and Marla had not gotten lost in the crowd. The couple was walking arm in arm, both wearing baseball caps and sunglasses to hide their identities.

To Nancy the HG Studios Theme Park sparkled like a new toy. There was a festive air despite the announcement on the news the previous night that Irwin Gold's son had been arrested.

Outside the facade of the new ride, crowds were gathered to watch the opening. Sonia Gold was speaking with reporters, and Irwin Gold held a giant pair of scissors, preparing to cut the ribbon draped across the entrance. As Frank studied the bright, sharp eyes of the film mogul, he recalled the conversation they'd had in Gold's office the day before.

"I never suspected a traitor in my own house," Irwin Gold had told the Hardys, shaking his head regretfully. "My son and daughter have always been competitive. When Jason kept pushing for the Twinkle deal, I simply thought it was another way of outshining his sister. None of us knew the extent of Jason's problem."

"Not to mention the fact that he enlisted an accomplice," Joe had pointed out. Jason had admitted to paying off Ken Zubin to maintain minimal security at the park. As a result, both Ken and Jason had been arrested. Although Ken Zubin faced minor charges, Jason would be in prison for a long time.

"I'm eternally grateful to you boys for weeding our garden," Mr. Gold had told the Hardys.

Frank's attention snapped back to the entrance of Haunted Holiday, where Irwin Gold cut the ribbon amid a round of applause. Then the small man went to the podium, thanked the crowd for attending, and introduced "the creative mind behind Haunted Holiday, Ms. Zoe Fortune!"

"That's a new twist," Nancy said as she clapped for the tall woman draped in a caftan of rich African fabrics. Zoe bowed to the crowd with a dramatic flourish.

"Mr. Gold had a change of heart," Frank explained. "He read over her original script and realized that she did deserve credit. He settled the lawsuit with Zoe Fortune out of court and agreed to involve her in today's presentation. Though he's playing the magnanimous studio exec, I think Mr. Gold is hoping that Zoe's colorful personality will distract the press—give them something positive to write about the park."

"Now that the truth about Jason is out, does Mr. Gold think it will hurt business?" Nancy asked.

"He speculates that attendance at the park may drop off a bit, but he and Sonia are committed to the entertainment business. The deal with Twinkle is off. The Golds are sticking with the theme park and studio for the long haul."

"Are you guys ready to ride Haunted Holiday?" Bess asked.

"Don't forget," Joe said, "we've got our VIP passes."

"Let's go!" Marla said. "I'm in the mood for a good scare. Although from now on, I'm happy to say, there won't be so many scares in my personal life. Thanks to you, Nancy."

"I'm just glad that we caught Chelsea before she could do serious harm," Nancy said.

"Me, too," Tony agreed, giving Marla a quick kiss.

The group went in through the VIP entrance and found themselves in the dimly lit lobby, where babbling trolls swooped down over them, their rubbery fingers dangling just inches from the top of Nancy's head.

"Ooh, how creepy!" Bess said, using the eerie creatures as an excuse to cuddle close to Zeke.

"Don't worry," Zeke said as they lined up on the platform waiting for the coffin-shaped cars to arrive. "I'll protect you from all those things that go bump in the night."

A zombie with missing teeth and stringy white hair greeted them, then helped Bess, Zeke, Marla, and Tony into the first coffin. As soon as they were whisked down the track, the zombie looked up and flashed Nancy, Joe, and Frank a menacing smile that made Nancy's skin crawl.

"Joe? Is that you?" the zombie asked.

"Yeah," Joe said, eyeing her cautiously.

"It's me! Randi Jo!" she said brightly. "I saw you on the news last night. You're a detective! And you never said a word. I didn't suspect a thing when I was training you."

"My brother and I were undercover," Joe explained, warming to her despite her hideous costume.

"Well, congratulations on solving your case," she said as their coffin pulled up. "You may have saved our park."

"No problem," Joe said, stepping into the coffin behind Nancy and Frank. "Say, maybe we can get together later today? When you're on break?"

She shrugged, and for a moment her dimples showed through her makeup. "Sure. And you can tell me all about your case. Uh, that is"—her voice deepened ghoulishly—"if you survive the horrors of Haunted Holiday."

"We'll make it," Joe said, flashing her a smile. "Though as I remember it, that vampire ahead has a nasty bite."

EAU CLAIRE DISTRICT LIBRARY